MW01001021

SPIDER

Spider
Copyright © 2017 by Ilsa Madden-Mills
Little Dove Publishing

ISBN-13:978-1979450171
ISBN-10:197945017X

Cover Design by:
Shanoff Designs

Model: Amadeo Leandro

Photography: Wong Sim

Editing:
Caitlin with Editing by C. Marie

Interior Design & Formatting by:
Christine Borgford, Type A Formatting

AUTHOR'S NOTE

This is a full-length standalone *loosely based* on a short story I wrote in 2013. This short story, and I mean short, appeared in two anthologies: *Breakaway* and *Beaus and Arrows*, both of which are now unavailable for purchase.

Flawed, broken, and utterly gorgeous, Spider's been talking with a British accent in my head for years.

Now, he's all yours . . . I hope you love him.

Ilsa

SPIDER

From *Wall Street Journal* best-selling author Ilsa Madden-Mills comes a standalone romance about a flawed hero and the woman he can't forget.

He calls himself Spider.

I just knew him as the sinfully gorgeous guy with eyes of fire that fate put next to me on the airplane.

I didn't know who he *really* was . . . future rock star . . . my stepbrother.

He kissed me because he thought we'd never see each other again. We would.

Everyone warned me about him.

They said he was ruthless and screwed up.

That he'd leave me with a hole in my heart.

Maybe I should have listened.

Maybe I should have built up a fortress to keep him out.

But I crumbled instead.

They say an unbreakable thread connects those who are destined to meet. If that's true, then the moment he sat next to me, we were bound together forever.

He just had to figure it out before it's too late . . .

SPIDER

Wall Street Journal Bestselling Author
ILSA MADDEN-MILLS

PART I

One often meets his destiny on the road he takes to avoid it.

ONE

Rose

Before

A FLASH OF LIGHTNING CRISSCROSSES the ceiling of my bedroom, and I jerk awake in the darkness. Mama's been playing loud music all night, but it's the storm that startles me, its rumble shaking the walls inside our tiny house in a rundown neighborhood outside of Dallas, Texas. Commonly referred to as Tin Town because of its junkyards, recycling centers, and used car lots, it's a hotbed of poverty and crime. How do I know this if I'm only eleven? Because I watch the news, thank you very much. Sometimes I even see my street on there when someone gets shot or mugged.

Dripping sounds reach my ears, and I watch as a small trickle of water slides down my wall. A big gust of wind blew shingles off the roof last spring, making the ceiling leak in the corner of my room. Mama said she was going to get the landlord to fix it, but she never did.

A man's deep voice carries over the sound of "Hotel California" by the Eagles, and my heart dips.

All thoughts of going back to sleep vanish.

I know that voice well. It's Mama's boyfriend Lyle—or *piece of shit*, as Granny liked to call him.

He comes around every now and then and gets Mama riled up. They fight like cats and dogs, tearing at each other with their fists and hurling insults, and then just as hurriedly they make up and kiss each other.

From out in the hall, it sounds like they are arguing, and I stiffen, the air crackling with a weird energy. Maybe it's the storm beating against the house or the dark timbre of his voice, but something is off. I hear Mama cackle like she does when she's high, and fear prickles over me, sending tingles all the way to my scalp.

Granny always said I had good instincts and that I'd inherited her ability to read people, and I trust it now.

Time to hide.

Scrambling out of my covers, I scoot under my small bed, pushing dust bunnies out of the way. Clutched to my chest is a stuffed teddy Granny gave me before she died.

There's scuffling at my door.

Whispers.

My fear ratchets up.

"Just let me look at her," I hear him say to Mama. "I won't hurt her."

"She's asleep. Leave her alone," Mama says in her sly way, and I picture her running her hands across his chest like she does before they go to the bedroom.

She's trying to distract him from me, either because she cares about me, or because she's jealous. I never know her motives; she's one of the few people I can't read.

"Come on," he cajoles in a teasing voice. "Let me see your pretty girl. I want to see how she's grown." His tone is light, but there's darkness there, a quality to it that makes the hair on my arms stand straight up.

I do *not* want him to come in my room.

I know what men like him want.

I see the way he looks at me.

He says I have legs long enough to wrap around a stripper pole.

Granny warned me that one day he'd come for me too.

The doorknob rattles.

Run!

Scrambling on my hands and knees, I fly out from under the bed and crawl to the window beside it. Jagged streams of lightning flash outside as I shove the glass up and heave myself to the sill, perching for half a second before jumping. I land in a mud puddle at the bottom, streaks of brown splashing up my bare legs.

The wind whips at me as I run, aiming for the skinny pine trees behind the house. Looking over my shoulder, I see a light click on in my bedroom and hear Mama calling my name. I hear his voice, angry and hard, as he shouts at me from the window.

His tone fills my stomach with ice.

I dart behind a log and hunker down, shaking as the storm batters from above.

They never come for me.

HOURS LATER, I BLINK MY eyes open as the sun comes up. I want to go back home, but sometimes Lyle stays for days until he gets tired of Mama.

In the low light of morning, I walk along a trail through the woods to the Quickie Mart on the main road. My intent is clear: steal something to eat. I've done it before, a bag of chips here, a candy bar there.

I see the rusty green dumpster in the back parking lot and come to a halt, my senses on high alert, watching as a wad of money and a brown package are exchanged between a teenage boy with tousled white hair and a known drug dealer in the neighborhood.

I can't look away.

The teenager is new to me, beautiful with high cheekbones that perfectly accentuate his straight nose and full lips. He wears a pair of clean jeans that make me envious and a tightly fitted black turtleneck that makes his white hair pop. His hair is so shiny and styled, I imagine he spends more time fixing it than I take in the entire morning when I shower and get ready for school. An expensive looking leather jacket completes the outfit. He looks like a movie star and obviously doesn't belong in this neighborhood.

I should at least hide in the tall weeds since it's a drug deal, but I don't, immobilized by how different he is from anyone I've ever met, from his thickly lashed eyes to the way his shoulders shrug effortlessly as he talks.

I analyze him like I do everyone, filing him away in the cabinet of my mind: handsome, arrogant, rich, *trouble.*

His face turns directly toward me, dark eyes lasering in on my own. Faster than lightning, I drop down in the weeds, heart flying.

Minutes tick by slowly as I crouch in the rain-soaked grass. Finally, I hear a car start and pull away. Relief rushes through me. Last year one of the kids from my school witnessed a drug deal and bragged about it, telling us every single detail down to names.

About a week later, he just disappeared, and no one knows what happened to him.

I wait, counting to a hundred before I stand.

I get to fifty when a pair of expensive tennis shoes appear in front of me.

"Hiya. You looking for bugs down there?" the beautiful guy says, his accent weird.

I blink up at him. "I didn't see a thing."

He does that shrug thing, the one where your eyes automatically go to his chest. It's a nice chest as far as I can tell. He isn't beefed up like a football player—I can take him if I have to.

"Don't care what you saw. What's your name?"

"I'm no one important," I say tersely, daring him to dispute it.

His lips twitch. "Nice to meet you, *No One Important*. How's about you stand up and let me see you?"

I maneuver to my feet and face him.

He arches a brow at my bare legs and sleep shirt.

I tug at the hem of the fabric, hoping it covers my butt. It does—barely. I must look like a drowned rat.

He purses his lips, brown eyes studying me intently, making me squirm. I think I see a flash of compassion on his face. "Let me guess—you ran away from home?"

My lips tighten. I'm not telling him jack. I can knee a boy in the nuts in two seconds flat and then run like the wind if I have to.

He looks around the parking lot. "Things might be tough at home, kiddo, but this isn't a good place for you. Stuff goes down back here, ya know what I mean? A girl could get in some big trouble."

I squint at him. *Does he think I'm slow?*

Of course this place is dangerous.

My whole world is.

"You got somewhere to go? Somebody you want me to call?" His eyes sweep over the teddy bear I grabbed on the way out. I tug it closer to my chest.

"I'm hungry," comes out of me.

He sighs heavily and scrubs his face, his expression thoughtful as he bends down to me. Out from his pocket comes another wad of money like the one I saw before. He peels off three bills. "Here. Take this and get yourself some food—and don't waste it on candy. Get some protein in you. You're skinny."

I eye the money suspiciously even as my fist clutches it tight. I've never seen a hundred-dollar bill, much less *three* at one time. It's enough to keep me in candy bars for months.

"What do you want from me?" I know what happens when men give women money. They always want something in return.

He frowns again and sticks his hands in his pockets. "Nothing. Just get something to eat, and if things get tough at home, call the police okay?"

"Police ain't any good. They'll just put me in a home, and it might be one that's even *worse*." I give him my *you must be an idiot* look.

"I ran away a few times too, kid. Been there."

"Yeah, so?" I shrug.

He laughs at me, and I stare up at him, fascinated once again. The more he talks in that weird accent, the more I want to look at him. I check out the skull ring on his finger, the swirl of a tattoo that peeks out from the sleeve of his turtleneck. He *looks* like a bad man, but he isn't—even if he is in the back lot of the Quickie Mart.

It's the heart that always knows, and mine does.

"How old are you?" I blurt out.

He grins at me with a flash of even white teeth. "Sixteen."

"I'm eleven." I spear him with a look. "Do you dye your hair that color? It's awfully white. At first I thought you might be an albino, but your eyes are the wrong color and your skin isn't pale."

He tosses back his head and laughs . . . like he's untouchable and owns the world.

My stomach rumbles.

He sobers. "You need to eat."

I shrug. It doesn't help that I went to bed hungry.

"Why are you looking at me?" I ask after a few moments of his watching me.

He shakes his head, as if bemused. "I don't know. You intrigue me, and I'm bored."

I indicate the bulge in his side pocket. "You got your drugs. What's keeping you in Tin Town?"

He scratches his head, and we have a bit of a stare-off.

"Give me your arm," he says a few ticks later as he steps closer to me.

I flinch, an old habit, and take a solid step away from him. "No."

He holds his hands up in a placating manner then pulls a pen out of his jacket pocket. "I'm not going to hurt you . . . just let me give you my digits in case you get in some big trouble, okay?"

I nod, watching him warily as he eases in closer, picks up my arm, and writes the numbers across my forearm: 555–481–9066. "That's my mobile number."

"It's called a cell, and if I ever get one, I'll call you," I say coolly, trying to play older than I am. "Might be a while. I'm not rich, you know."

His lips kick up again and he shakes his head. "You remind

me of someone."

I cock my head. "Who?"

"No One Important." He pauses, his face rueful. "Me."

I smile.

"You'll be okay, right? Will you call me if you need help?"

"Yeah."

He nods and saunters away from me, walking backward as if he wants to keep his eyes on me the entire time.

But it isn't a weird, sleazy look like Lyle has when he watches me; no, it's more . . . as if he doesn't know what category to put me in.

I get that.

I put everyone in a category.

I have a nose for it.

Lyle—bad. Granny—good. Mama—who the hell knows.

Beautiful Guy is one of the good ones.

Maybe he thinks I am too.

A warm flush colors my face.

"Where are you from?" I call out to him as the distance between us increases. I don't want him to go.

"Across the pond," he replies with a jaunty wave as he walks toward a black Jeep with wheels so shiny and crisp they glitter in the sun. He sends me one last look and cranks the car up, rap music blaring as he spins out of the lot.

I miss him immediately.

After devouring a bag of chicken tenders and two candy bars, I make my way back along the trail, my thoughts still on him.

He gave me money and wanted *nothing* in return.

Who knew such people existed?

I come to the tree line and my window is still up, the curtains blowing idly in the soft wind. Walking around to the front, I see that Lyle is gone already. I ease open the door and step into the den. The room smells like stale cigarettes and old food. I take in the overturned coffee table, the broken vase, and the bottles of beer littering the floor.

I've seen this before.

It's fine.

She's fine.

I find Mama behind the couch, her head cocked at a weird angle, her blank eyes staring up at me, reminding me of a dead fish from the market.

She's scary.

My breathing changes, coming faster.

"Mama?" My hand grips the armrest on the couch.

"*Mama?*"

I inch toward her, touch her hand, and jerk back at her cold skin.

I drop my bag of food and scream as loud as I can.

Until my throat is raw.

Until tears run down my face.

Until the police run in the door.

And later, nothing falls into place until fate tiptoes in and sets me on my path.

Until I see *him* again . . .

TWO

Spider

Six years later

BUGGER ME.

Not only does my head pound, but I'm striking out big time with a lady old enough to be my nana.

The neatly dressed gate agent crosses her arms. She's sick of me. Most women get to that point eventually.

"Sir, you can't carry your guitar on. You'll need to check it."

"Make an exception for me? *Please*, Betty?" I say, glancing at her nametag and accentuating the English accent. Usually, my clipped tones get me out of sticky situations, especially with the female half of the population, but I've been hitting a brick wall since the moment I walked up to the desk. Maybe it's my tattoos, leather jacket, and mesh tank top—I don't exactly scream *nice guy*.

Her beady eyes sweep over me, lingering on the black widow artwork on my neck and then moving to check out my hair. I touch it self-consciously. It's cobalt blue this month, swept back in a gelled pompadour style with the sides shaved close to my scalp. Next week, I'm dying it white. No matter the color, girls go nuts over it.

Not Betty.

"I'm sorry, but you already have a carry-on bag and a personal item. That's all that's allowed on the plane. Those are the rules, and they're clearly marked." She points to a sign on the wall next to me that explains the rules for flying with Delta. It's the second time she's pointed them out to me, and the stubborn arsehole I am, I refuse to look.

"But this is my one true love." I lightly stroke the case.

"It's a guitar," she says dryly.

I lift the case up on the counter and pop open the metal snaps, giving her a view of the yellow and blue instrument. "She's a Gibson Les Paul that's gutsy as shit but lightweight at the same time. She's made from maple with rosewood inlays—the best money can buy, worth over five grand. Paid for this baby myself. Dear old Dad didn't even help." I point to a small horizontal strip at the end of the fingerboard on the neck of the guitar. "See this here? That's the nut on the bass and it controls the string placement. It's made from *real bone*. I don't know what kind of bone it is, but I like to think it's from a lion or a tiger. Of course, they weren't killed to make the guitar, but their bones were donated after they died in some majestic battle in the wild. Fitting, right?" I grin.

Come on, Betty, let us on the plane, my eyes beg.

But Betty bristles at me, her bushy gray eyebrows lowered in a scowl behind tiny reading glasses. Her lips thin as she gazes down at the beautiful piece of art. "Please remove your item from my desk, sir."

I lean over the counter, widening my eyes, giving her the full-on Spider effect, or in other words: my gorgeous peepers with long black eyelashes. People tell me it's a gaze that's devastating to the female reproductive organs, and I question if she has working anatomy because she doesn't seem fazed by my allure, even when I bite my lip. "Helene and I—that's her name, Helene—have been together since I was fourteen."

"That's nice." She's already looking over my shoulder at the person behind me.

I forge on, lying through my teeth. "My girlfriend dumped me while I was here in New York." The truth is it's not hard to fake feeling low with a massive hangover. "She always had a cheating problem. Once it was my cousin she slept with—talk about some weird family get-togethers after that." I sigh. "We came here to, you know, figure things out, and then she met *him*."

"Look, Mr.—"

"Please, call me Spider."

Her brows shoot straight up, her eyes bouncing back to the black widow tattoo on my neck. "Er, Mr. Spider, I'm sorry about your girlfriend. She sounds awful, but—"

"Have you ever been cheated on, Betty?"

She nods, albeit a little grudgingly.

I wave my hands at her. "You get it then—the heartbreak. God, the way she played me."

"Was it your cousin again?"

I nod, dabbing at my eyes with a napkin I tucked in my pocket last night at the club. I peek at Betty, watching as she moves from foot to foot, her eyes weighing me, checking for sincerity.

"My dog died last week, too," I toss out in a last-ditch effort, sinking to a whole new low for me.

The thing is, I'm headed to see my father, and just the thought of seeing him makes me want to puke. He'll see what kind of shape

I'm in and know the truth.

I need help.

But also . . . *fuck him.*

"What kind of dog?" Betty asks, startling me.

What kind of dog?

Shit. I freeze, unable to snatch a breed of dog out of thin air. *Think of a dog! It's not that hard. What's that multicolored collie that had its own show in the seventies? Ah, my head. God, hangovers suck.*

"Say Yorkie," a female voice hisses in my ear from behind, the push of her words causing tingles to slide down my spine as she breathes against my neck. "They're cute and small. She'll like those. Plus, I'd *really* appreciate if you'd get out of my way so I can get on my plane. You've been holding up this line forever. It's rude."

The girl's warmth leaves me as she takes a step back.

I feel summarily dismissed.

"Collie," I say to a waiting Betty. "Like in *Lassie*, the TV show."

"I like Yorkies myself," Betty murmurs as she taps on her computer.

"Told you so," grumbles the voice of the girl behind me.

I ignore her and place our latest CD on the desk, signing it quickly with a permanent marker from my backpack. "Someday I'm going to be famous, and this is my gift to you, and I'm not giving you this so you'll take care of Helene . . . it's because you're a beautiful woman, Betty, and every beautiful woman deserves a little surprise in her day." My lips kick up in a grin. "But, if you can find a way to get my guitar on the plane, well, that would just be icing on the cake. Maybe I'll write a song about you—Betty has quite the ring to it."

Lo and behold, a dimple appears on each of her cheeks as she takes the CD and gives me a considerably warmer look. "We have an area in first class that we usually reserve for coats and such. Maybe there's room there. Let me check."

Two seconds later she's calling someone up, checking if they have a place for my guitar.

I smell victory.

Something soft pokes me in the back.

"What the—" I turn and see a large bed pillow currently being held by the girl who whispered in my ear. I move my gaze up and take her in.

Ruby red lips.

A tight black dress.

And a pair of high-top red Converse.

Damn. I bite my lip—and this time, it isn't fake.

Pillow Girl checks *all* my boxes.

I half-expected some uptight old lady in a nun habit, but she doesn't look old, maybe somewhere in the vicinity of my own age of twenty-two. She's gorgeous in a way that makes guys—and girls—look twice, maybe three times, but I see beautiful babes all the time on the road.

Wide eyes stare back at me, landing on my tattoo and then dropping down to take in my shoulders, hips, and legs. I smile widely because I know I look tight. My face is near perfect, my shoulders are muscled, and my long legs look damn good in designer jeans.

"Sorry I poked you," she says with an arch to her brow.

Somehow I don't think she's sorry. I think she was trying to get my attention.

I smile. "Ever fancy trying a neck pillow instead of that jumbo-sized thing?" I nod my head at her large, fluffy accessory. "They're small and travel quite well. You can even purchase one in the airport."

Full, perfect-as-fuck lips tighten. "I happen to like my pillow."

I pause as a wave of déjà vu washes over me. There's something about her face . . .

I cock my head. "Do I know you?"

She shakes her head but she doesn't look sure.

I squint. "Are you sure we haven't hooked up before?"

"We haven't," she says curtly. "I saw your band in Greenwich Village last night."

Ah, the bar next to New York University. It had been a sold out show, and I didn't get out of there until three in the morning.

I nod. "Shame. I don't remember you."

She shrugs. "I'm not surprised. You were covered up in girls."

"We can get to know each other on the plane?" I ask, cocking an eyebrow in her direction.

She blinks as if I flustered her and it makes me grin.

"You aren't my type."

"Too bad," I murmur. "You're mine."

Her eyes flare.

Betty hangs up the phone. "Good news! You can take the guitar on. There's a flight attendant on board named Heidi who'll be looking for you."

Finally.

I grin broadly as Betty scans my pass, and with a sardonic *Cheerio* to the babe, I saunter off to board the plane, my thoughts on seeing my father for the first time in six months. He's summoned me to his home in Highland Park, outside of Dallas, where he's starting a whole new life. He wants me to meet his new wife where we can pretend to be one big happy family.

Whatever.

If I want his money, I have to play by his rules.

I WALK DOWN THE JET-WAY and stop at the entrance to the plane, where a flight attendant is greeting the passengers.

"Heidi?" I say, my lips tipping up at the curvy redhead in the typical navy skirt and heels.

She smiles back, checking me out. "You must be the owner of the guitar."

"Indeed."

She laughs. "Great. I'll just stow this in the coat closet in first class for you. You can grab it on your way out when we land." Her smile widens. "Adore your accent. You in a band?"

I nod. "Yeah. Vital Rejects. Ever heard of us?"

She gives me a blank stare.

"Yeah, we're nobody—at the moment."

She flicks a strand of hair over her shoulder. "I'll be sure to check on you quite often," she says, her lips curving up. "If you need a blanket or a pillow—"

"Good grief, don't you *ever* stop flirting? Just please move over. You're blocking the way for everyone," calls an annoyed voice from behind me.

Pillow Girl.

Damn, she's everywhere.

I watch in amusement as she weasels past me, her bottom brushing against my crotch as she huffs and carries on down the aisle.

Her heart-shaped ass sways from side to side in her black dress. She has to be at least five eleven, and that isn't even in heels. Her legs are tan and smooth and long—

Someone bumps into me as I watch her, and I scoot over to give the passengers coming onto the plane more room.

"Would you like to meet the pilot?" Heidi asks me, her smile flirtatious.

"Delta is my favorite airline," I say.

She giggles and introduces me to the pilot, and I end up giving both of them a copy of our CD and a quick spiel about our music. I sign them both, and before I know it, two other flight attendants are crowding into the cockpit area, insisting on a copy.

I smile at them, used to the attention.

One girl slyly tucks her business card in the back pocket of my jeans as she pats my ass.

I smirk at her and waggle my eyebrows.

She and Heidi exchange a few whispered words, and it's obvious she's warning the other girl that I've already been claimed.

I chuckle.

Sebastian Tate, our lead singer and my best mate since my prep school days in Highland Park, jokes that I have a way about me that sucks people in. His theory is it's the accent, but mostly it's my *party like the world is ending* attitude. I'm the mate everyone wants. Hell, I'm the guy who volunteers to do the beer run (and pays for it) then comes back with a case of tequila and a carload of beautiful women.

Live fast and collect no hearts is my mantra.

I'm fearless.

After all, I have nothing in life to lose, not when I've already lost it all.

I shove those dark thoughts away, blaming them on my pounding head. *Fuck hangovers.* I just need a bump of pure white bliss to get me over the edge.

After cheek-kissing the flight attendants, I head to my seat and see that my seatmate has already arrived—and guess who it is?

She's still just as hot as before.

I halt and stare down at her, surprised when I catch a gander at what I see on her Kindle: *100 Foolproof Rules To Get A Man To Fall In Love With You.*

I grin.

Is the girl trying to get a bloke?

Oh yeah.

This flight isn't going to feel nearly as long as I expected after all.

You know the old adage of turning lemons into lemonade? Pillow Girl is my lemon, and I'm going to turn her into the sweetest drink ever.

THREE

Rose

I WALK DOWN THE AIRPLANE aisle and eyeball the window seat I've been assigned. Three, maybe four inches separate me from death.

Yeah, I'm tough, but flying makes me crazy scared.

Planes are basically just battered tin coffins traveling a million miles an hour. Toss in a small thunderstorm—like the one currently surrounding us—and I'm a freaking basket case. Sweat beads on my forehead as I picture my mangled body on the ground amid flaming debris.

My hands tremble as I unpack my backpack, removing my lucky paperback copy of *Jane Eyre*, my Kindle—you can't have too many books—and a sweater. I'm freezing on this plane, and I'm not sure if it's from nerves or if it's actually cold. *Nerves*, I decide as I furtively check out the other passengers who seem warm and toasty.

Shivering, I settle in my seat and try to read the ridiculous book my cousin Marge has downloaded to my Kindle. A twenty-something New Yorker, I stayed with her while I visited New York University on my spring break from prep school. We had some late-night talk sessions, and when I mentioned my crush Trenton back in Highland Park, she made it her mission to load me up with self-help books and advice about how to get the man of your dreams.

It's a dumb idea, and I know it.

But it's hard to tell Marge no.

Forgetting the book, I lean my head back against the headrest on the seat. I'm tired from my evening out with her, even though I sat in the corner at the back of the bar and just watched everyone most of the night. I was nervous since I'm only seventeen and used a fake ID, which Marge provided. I'll be eighteen in September, about five months from now.

My thoughts go back to the hot guy from the gate.

From the moment I first saw him last night, something about him just . . . called to me.

It was as if I knew him—yet I didn't.

My eyes followed him the entire night, the way he stalked across the stage as if he was fearless, the way his lean and muscular body whipped around, moving with the rhythm of his gritty and evocative music. With an excuse to Marge that I had to go to the bathroom, I'd even followed him outside during the break where I watched from the doorway as he smoked a cigarette, leaning his head against the brick of the building as he blew smoke up into the air. He hadn't noticed me . . . of course. There'd been too many girls around him vying for his attention. In a nutshell, he was way out of my league.

Forget about him.

Right.

What I should be doing is focusing on convincing my adoptive mother Anne to let me attend NYU this fall.

As if she knew I was thinking about her, my phone pings with a text from her.

Did Marge behave herself? Growing up, she was quite wild.

From Anne, this really means she thinks Marge is a slut. I was actually surprised when she agreed to let me visit Marge, and I attribute her acquiescence to her own recent surprise pregnancy and subsequent hasty marriage. That's right. My uptight, forty-five-year-old adoptive mom had a one night stand and got pregnant.

I type out a reply. **She was great. Very hospitable. Her apartment is close to NYU.**

Her reply is quick and fast, and I picture her fingers typing the words furiously. She hates any mention of NYU and every time I bring up attending there, she shuts me down.

I know NYU seems exciting, but Winston University is smaller and here in town. Plus, you've been accepted. It's too late to apply to NYU. Only a few more weeks and you'll be graduating high school. Love, Anne

Only Anne texts as if it were a term paper, with complete sentences and correct punctuation.

I sigh, my fingers running idly over the surface of my phone. I don't want to attend Winston. Exclusive and located just ten minutes from Highland Park, it's just like the prep school I currently attend, only with older students. It's also where Anne went to college. I mean, I'm grateful she's providing me with an education, but I'd like to have a say in the matter.

She's under the impression that this trip was just a quick visit to see her cousin and take in the sights on spring break. She doesn't know that I secretly already applied to NYU months ago and recently got the acceptance letter. I just have to talk her into it.

A well-known Dallas philanthropist, I first met Anne after two years of being shuffled around in the foster system. That day, she'd sat with me in the office at the Department of Human Services and marveled over my hair color (a mix of brown and auburn) and complimented me on my perfect skin. I read her right away, a rich lady looking for an accessory, and I used it to my advantage, telling her about my above average test scores and my dream of getting a doctorate in psychology someday.

It worked, and once she took me in and adopted me, I was given a complete makeover: a new layered hair cut with a tutorial on how to style it, conservative clothing, and a course on manners and etiquette. Want to know where the water glass should be at a place setting? Just ask me . . . approximately one inch from the tip of the dinner knife. She molded me into her idea of what a perfect girl should be.

I sigh as guilt tugs at me for going to the bar in New York . . . for even wanting to attend NYU. She's given me so much, and I shouldn't want to get away from her, but I can't breathe in Highland Park. With famous residents such as past Presidents, country music celebrities, and Texas bigwigs, I simply don't belong in the wealthy suburb.

Before we have to turn our phones on airplane mode, another text comes in, this time from Trenton.

Butterflies go crazy in my stomach as I read it.

Senior Spring Fling is coming up. Wanna go?

Senior Spring Fling is a notoriously secret party sponsored by the popular kids at Claremont Prep and held the first weekend in May, usually at a destination that's only revealed at the last possible moment. If you don't get the invite, you're a nobody—which

I am. I don't really care about going, but Trenton is popular and attractive, and I'd be crazy to tell him no.

Yes, I reply then quickly lock my phone before I say anything else like, *Is this a friend thing or a date thing?*

He and I have been flirting with each other for a while . . .

Whatever. I can figure all that out later.

Glancing up from my seat, I see Spider—yes, I know his name from the bar last night—stalking down the aisle like a Greek god. Wearing expensive black jeans with holes in the knees, motorcycle boots, and a gray leather jacket, he has major bad boy vibes all over him.

Completely dangerous.

Completely panty-melting.

Not going to lie, he has the kind of face that takes your breath and stops you in your tracks. Just looking at him straight on makes me blush. He isn't classically handsome like Trenton, with his square chin and athletic shoulders. Instead, he grabs your attention with his hollowed cheeks, the sharp edges along his jawline, and the thick black lashes that surround his eyes.

He comes to a halt right next to my seat and props his muscular forearms on the overhead bin. He's lean yet toned with sharply defined muscles, his height at least six three. My breath hitches when his gaze lands on mine. He stares at me, and I don't look away. Warm and honey-colored, his eyes are pools of sunlight shining through whiskey. I could get drunk in those pools.

Oh . . . wait. I blink.

He's sitting here? *With me?*

Sweet baby Jesus. I'm a goner.

Stay strong, Rose.

I tuck my Kindle down into the seat.

He smirks, his eyes following me, and I grimace, realizing he probably saw what I was reading.

"Great," he says. "I get to sit next to Pillow Girl."

Ignoring the nickname, I shrug. "And I get to sit by the guy who lies to little old ladies about his girlfriend dumping him—and we can't forget the poor dead collie you recently lost. And dabbing at your eyes with that napkin—great touch."

I don't know why I'm so annoyed with him.

Yes, you do.

I exhale. Okay, I do. I really wish he remembered me from the bar. I wish he were as fascinated by me as I was by him. Last night after his show, I even dreamed of him and this morning when I woke up, he was the first thing on my mind. Strange.

What was it about him that pricked at me? I don't know.

His lips twitch. "I nearly cocked that whole thing up. I'm not exactly at the top of my game today."

"I bet you've never even had a dog." I smile, softening the words as I study his profile, tracing the lines of a face that's flawlessly heartbreaking. It's hard to stay annoyed with someone so damned gorgeous.

He chuckles as he eases into the space and sits down. "I did, a huge mastiff named Noodles. My sister and I used to ride him like a pony, and he loved every minute of it." He buckles his seat belt and I find myself watching his long fingers, noticing how elegant they are. I recall how those very fingers strummed his guitar the night before. I can't help but imagine them on my skin as warmth settles throughout everything below my navel.

Get a grip, Rose. He's too old for you.

"I'm not sure I can trust a thing you say after the lies you told Betty," I say.

He shrugs. "True story. The sad part is my father sold him along with our estate when we moved to the US. I often wonder what happened to the big lug."

Estate? He must be rich.

"What brought you to the US? Music?" I'm curious about what makes him tick.

Something flashes beneath the controlled expression of nonchalance he wears, and I stare at him intensely, trying to catch the minute shift in his emotions. He lets out a sigh as his fingers tap nervously on his thighs. "My father wanted out of London, kind of like a fresh start for us."

Interesting. I'm itching to ask him *why* the fresh start, but common sense tells me it's too personal.

"Noodles is a cute name. There must be a story there?"

A quick grin ghosts over his face. "When he was a pup, he'd never beg for scraps. Father had him trained by a puppy school so he knew how to behave, but if Cook ever served a Bolognese sauce with spaghetti—all bets were off. No admonishing or collar zapping would make him stop barking until you put a few in his bowl." He tosses his head back and laughs. "So, we changed his name to Noodles. Much better than Bertram, am I right?" His gaze slides to me, amusement making the hard lines of his face soft.

No man has the right to be that freaking hot.

I swallow, feeling all of seventeen and completely out of my element. "Yeah. Totally."

My usually adept vocabulary is sadly missing.

"You got pets?" he asks as his eyes linger on my face. "I bet you're a cat person."

"Why would you say that?"

He smirks. "You're a little prickly . . . like a cat with an attitude."

Oh. The way he says the word *cat*, like he likes it, makes me feel . . . fluttery. "I love all animals, but I live on campus at the moment." The student dorms are a recent thing for me since Anne married and then promptly left for a month long honeymoon. I insisted I would be okay at their house in Highland Park until they returned, but she was adamant that I move into school housing where there was some supervision. Since Anne is on the school board, the administration agreed to let me move in until graduation.

"Ah, a college girl."

I lie—or at least, I don't correct him. I nod and clear my throat as I change the topic. "Your band was amazing last night."

"Thank you. What song was your favorite?"

I loved all of their music, but a few stood out, especially a slow ballad called "Albatross" where Spider sang and played guitar. "The one about the guy lost at sea and all alone." I pause, feeling self-conscious as I think about the underlying theme of the song and how I related to it. "It was a retelling of the poem *The Rime of the Ancient Mariner*, right?"

He nods, looking thoughtful as he cocks his head and studies me. "Not everyone catches that."

I shrug. "I love literature and music. The song . . . it was about carrying your burdens around your neck? Did you write it?"

He blinks at me. "Yes to both. You're pretty astute." He gets quiet, and I can tell I touched a nerve. It's clear he doesn't want to get too deep.

He clears his throat. "Look, I'm sorry about holding up the line earlier . . . with Betty and the flight attendant."

I shrug. "I'm sorry for being so grouchy. Flying makes me weird."

"So we can start over?"

I nod, already over it since he sat down, and he smiles, an earnest expression growing on his face. "Since we're talking music, what did you think of my guitar solo on the song "Superhero"? Did you like the mink coat? It was fake, by the way. I'd never wear a real fur."

I grow warm, remembering flashes of his well-endowed package in a pair of leopard print bikini underwear as he strutted around in the long fur coat, an outfit he put on just for that song. Only someone with massive amounts of confidence could have worn that ensemble. "If your goal was for women to throw their panties at you—it worked."

He smiles sheepishly. "I'm hard to resist, but you never know. I like to get serious opinions."

I roll my eyes at his *hard to resist* comment, and he laughs.

He takes off his jacket and stretches out his long legs, and his scent drifts in my direction, cedar mixed with the smell of leather. It makes me a little giddy.

We're sitting incredibly close, and even though I know I shouldn't, I'm staring at him. He's just so different with the tattoos and blue hair. My eyes keep sneaking peeks over at him and taking mental notes. I study the word LOST tattooed on his left knuckles.

"You got a name?" he asks a few moments later as he settles his head back against his headrest.

"Primrose, but everyone calls me Rose."

"Nice. I fancy Rose . . . it's old-fashioned, but pretty." He smiles and it hits me straight in the heart . . . devilish, charming, and disarming all at once. His eyes drift lazily over my face, his gaze landing on my mouth and not budging.

My heart skips a beat, and I swallow.

Fact: if men stare at your mouth, they want to kiss you—or

you have really bad teeth.

Thanks to Anne, mine are perfectly straight.

But before I can formulate a reply to his comment, everything inside me freezes as the plane begins its taxi down the airstrip.

FOUR

Spider

WE RACE DOWN THE AIRSTRIP and lift into the air, the pressure making my ears pop. I glance over at Rose and see she's clutching the sides of her seat, her face deathly pale as we rise in altitude.

"You okay?" I ask softly, frowning at the loss of color in her cheeks.

She does an all-over body shiver, her throat moving as she swallows. "I hate flying—and storms. Plus, the window seat makes me queasy."

Shit. If I had known, I would have switched with her earlier. "You can have my seat once we get leveled out."

She shakes her head. "It's okay, I'm settled in now . . . just really cold."

I hate that she's cold. Once we get to cruising altitude and can unbuckle our seat belts, I signal to the nearby flight attendant to bring us a blanket.

Heidi brings the blanket, and I hand it to Rose.

"Thank you." She takes it, our hands briefly touching.

"That flight attendant likes you," she says, her eyes watching as Heidi sashays off. "She hasn't taken her eyes off of you since you boarded."

"She's not the one I want to like me," I murmur. It's rather abrupt and to the point, but I always say what I mean. Why waste time? I want Rose.

I watch her to gauge her reaction.

"Oh." A blush rises up her face as she busies herself by trying to make the short blanket cover her legs and chest area. I see right away that it's not going to work.

"Here, I have an idea." I reach under my seat, pull out my jacket, and arrange it over her torso. I lean over her to adjust it, hitching it up on her shoulder, as I cover her up.

She smiles softly and thanks me, making me blush—which is so weird.

I clear my throat. "I have to warn you though . . . this is my favorite jacket. Girls don't usually get to wear it, so you're pretty special. No drooling if you fall asleep, okay?"

She bites her lower lip, the one I can't stop looking at. "If I drool does that mean I get to keep it?"

"Depends."

"On what?" she says, and her voice has lowered.

"On what you're willing to do to get it."

Another silence fills the air between us as we stare at each other, but it's not weird or uncomfortable. It's hot and electric.

She breaks the tension by laughing. "I don't do anything I don't want to, so I guess you can keep it."

I laugh.

Damn. She isn't going to make this easy for me.

Feeling a bit flustered by her, I glance down at the Kindle she stuffed in the seat. With all our talk earlier and her fear of flying, I nearly forgot about it. I nudge my head at her Kindle and clear my throat. "I saw what you were reading. If you want to learn how to make a man fall in love with you, I can offer some advice."

She cocks her head. "Really? I hope it doesn't involve me wearing leopard print bikinis and mink coats."

"Touché."

She smirks, looking pleased, and it makes me want to kiss her.

"Who's the guy you're reading this for?"

She stiffens. "There's no guy."

"Un-uh. There's always a guy."

She sighs. "Okay, maybe there *is* a guy, but my cousin Marge actually bought this book."

"This dude, he isn't into you?"

"He's into a lot of girls, most of them popular—and I'm not."

Rose deserves a nice guy. I don't know *how* I know this, but I just do. "Maybe you should play hard to get."

"I don't play games."

"Ah, a girl after my own heart." I study her flawless skin, taking in the way her lashes flutter against her cheeks. Her long hair is twisted up in some kind of knot with wavy tendrils hanging around her face, and I picture how she'd look with it falling over her shoulders, caressing her naked tits . . .

She rearranges her blanket and her scent hits me, honey and vanilla mingled together. It's intoxicating, and I laugh off an odd nervousness, fighting the urge to press my nose against her neck and inhale.

Weird, Spider.

She clears her throat. "If I want something, I go after it."

"Maybe you should focus on someone else." *Like me, Mr. Next to You On The Plane Who Wants to Fuck You.*

She shrugs. "Maybe. He *is* hot."

Anger flares in my gut. I'm jealous. How . . . bloody silly.

"Is he as hot as I am?" I curl my arm, tightening my bicep for her.

She half-snorts. "You're charming, I'll give you that. No wonder poor Betty fell for it."

"Seriously though . . . is he?" I want to know—I *need* to know.

She stares at me, seeing that I'm serious. Her gaze lingers on my tattoos. "He's . . . different from you, more conservative." She waves her hands around. "He plays sports. You play guitar."

"Ah." At least now I know her type.

"Is the book working for you?" I ask.

"Haven't tried it."

"Then practice on me. Use some of those wiles from the book. Let me be your guinea pig, and I'll tell you if you suck."

Her eyes widen. You know that rich green color the ocean gets after a storm blows in? That's the color of her eyes. I lean in closer, taking in the gold around the inner parts of her irises. My finger touches the pout of her bottom lip. "How do you make a guy fall, Rose?" I murmur softly. "Tell me."

Her face goes red as she bites her bottom lip where I touched it. Her tongue darts out and licks the spot. She seems to find her equilibrium though as she clears her throat and leans over to whisper conspiratorially. *"Be provocative.* That's the one I just read. Pretty silly, right?"

My cock is hard as steel just from watching her lips say the word *provocative.* "Not at all," I say huskily. "Show me how you're provocative."

She shakes her head. "I don't even know you."

"Which makes it even better. We'll never see each other again."

"You'll laugh."

I grin. "I dare you."

Glowering, she considers me for a moment then reaches up and pulls her hair out of the bun it's in, creating a cascade of long brown hair around her face. Thick and wavy, different colors of autumn curl over her shoulders, making me want to pick up one of the strands and run my fingers through it. I picture her on a bed, her hair all spread out on a pillow . . .

I swallow down the lump in my throat. "Nice," I say as I sniff a strand. "Smells like vanilla. Not my personal favorite"—a lie—"but it works."

"You're too much."

"Not enough, never. What else you got? Throw it at me."

"Okay, how about this." She pulls a silver necklace out from her dress and strokes the chain as she simultaneously flicks her hair over her shoulder and sends me a heavy-lidded look. She bats those long lashes at me then chews on her bottom lip. It's a little silly—but I'm turned on.

"Hmmm, you're okay," I muse, feigning disinterest.

Her shoulders deflate. "Really? I mean, that's the best I have."

And it's fucking hot.

"Mind if I take a peek at the book?"

She hands it over and I skim a couple pages, checking out a list of to-dos.

1. *One word: laser. Remove all the hair from your body, including legs, armpits, and southern parts. No man likes hair unless he's a Neanderthal.*

2. *You know what guys hate? Small boobs. Get plastic surgery or give up ever finding a guy.*

I can't read anymore.

"Fascinating that people make money off this drivel," I say dryly.

"Trust me, I'm too smart to put any stock in it." She shakes her head ruefully. "Now I'm just embarrassed that you think I'm that stupid."

Clearing my throat, I dramatically read parts of them aloud. She giggles and tries to shush me, but I'm not having it. The other passengers have noticed and are staring.

Finally, with her face flaming in embarrassment, she pops me on the arm and jerks the Kindle out of my hand. "You've got to stop! No one on this plane wants to hear about breast augmentation."

"Oh, but I do." An idea comes to me. "Kiss me, Rose."

"What?" She blinks.

"*Kiss me.* I'm going to show you how to get your guy, and the first thing you need to know is how to use that gorgeous mouth of yours."

"Why?"

"Let me tell you a little secret," I say. "Getting your guy is mostly about what you don't say. Do you follow his every movement with your eyes? When you're walking together, are your steps in sync? When you come into a room, do his eyes go straight to you, even with beautiful women all around him? If the answer is no to any of those, then you're fucked. You can't change chemistry, and no amount of hair removal or fake boobs can create it. It just . . . is. Attraction is magic, and you can't find it in a book."

She seems to find my words fascinating. "What makes you

the expert on love?"

I wave her off—not even going there. "And your lips . . . they're perfect. That little indention you have right at the bottom is pure sex, but if you don't know how to use it properly . . ." My voice trails off.

"Okay."

"Okay, okay?" I arch a brow. "Is that a yes?" *Is she going to let me kiss her?*

She nods, and before she can finish the movement, I take her necklace, tug her face to mine, and lay one on her.

And this is the weird part: I haven't kissed a girl on the lips in a long time, but I go at it with her like I'm starving.

Her lips immediately part under mine, as if she's been waiting for this too. She tastes like sun-ripened cherries, and I delve deeper, exploring her. After a tentative few seconds, she gives it back, her tongue finding mine and tangling. It's gentle, but hot as hell. Cupping her face, I groan as I line her mouth with small feathery kisses, letting my teeth nip lightly on her bottom lip as I pull away.

"Spider," she says softly, her chest rising rapidly.

My dick's harder than I can ever remember, and all I want to do is kiss her again.

She moves closer to me, her tits pressing against my chest. My hand slips down to her neck and I graze the soft skin there, caressing her as I picture my lips sucking on her throat. I imagine my tongue playing with her nipples. Fuck. *I want her.*

"I want you," I say, my voice heavy with lust.

"Kiss me again," she says as I gaze into her eyes.

Damn. There's *something* about her—

A pocket of turbulence shakes the plane out of nowhere, and several passengers gasp and cry out.

I forget about kissing as fear flickers over her face and she clutches her seat once again. "Was that normal?"

"Just turbulence. The pilot will probably take us higher to get out of it," I say as the jarring continues.

Ding! The light to put on our seat belts comes on.

She closes her eyes, her voice high and reedy. "We're going to crash, aren't we? We're going to die."

"Hey." I grab her hand and lace our fingers together, wanting to comfort her. "It's going to be fine, I promise."

She looks down at our hands in surprise just as another bump sends a passenger stumbling on his way back from the bathroom.

She turns green as she folds herself into my chest. I wrap my arms around her shoulders. "It's okay, Rose."

When I get scared, my throat gets dry, so I look around for a flight attendant to get her some water. However, they've disappeared, probably buckling themselves in. I unclip my seat belt even though I'm not supposed to and stand to dig a bottle of water from my backpack, hanging on to the overhead so I don't fall. Once I find it, I quickly sit back down and hand it over to her.

"Thousands of planes take off and land every day," I say as she turns the bottle up.

"You're a musician, not an aerospace engineer." Her voice is a bit snappy.

I get it—she's terrified.

I understand that. I have my own hang-ups: I don't let people close to me.

"I happen to not like flying either. I just hide it very well." I take her hand again, intertwining our fingers.

She peeks over at me. "Really?"

I nod. "You know what else I'm scared of? Opening shower

curtains in every single hotel I stay in. I'm convinced there's going to be a knife-wielding psycho who looks like Dolly Parton waiting for me. Maybe it's the giant boobs, maybe it's the wig, but something about her scares me. Also, roaches with wings. I know I'm a grown man, but what if I try to kill the bugger and miss and then it comes back with all its friends at night and then crawls in my ear and messes with my brain?"

She smiles, just a hint. "Your imagination is limitless."

"Don't even get me started on zombies. I mean, what the hell is up with Americans and scary shows? Don't they know that someday scientists are going to reanimate people, and then what are we going to do? Send those walking skeletons to Mars?"

"I love *The Walking Dead*," she murmurs.

"You're a zombie-lover, just perfect."

"If we crash, let's come back as zombies."

"As long as we can be together, it's on, love." I raise a brow and watch as a slow blush starts at her neck and works its way up her face.

Something shifts between us, becoming softer and more intimate—even more so than the kiss. It feels fucking good. Relaxing for the first time in what seems like weeks of being on the road and doing shows, I lean my head back against the seat and stare at her, picking her features apart and trying to figure out which part I like the most.

Has to be the lips.

Or the red highlights in her hair.

No, it's definitely the way she looks at me with her eyes up and her chin slightly down, as if she doesn't quite know what to make of me.

"The turbulence stopped," she says, her eyes brightening as

she straightens in her seat and looks around the cabin.

I nod. "It stopped a few minutes ago while we were talking."

"Thank you for distracting me." She looks at the spider tattoo on my neck. "You have to tell me . . . how did you get a name like Spider?"

Her question sends me spinning in a whole new direction, careening toward darkness, but I push it back and focus on a happy memory. "It was my twin sister's name for me. Believe it or not, my natural hair color is almost black, and when I was young, I was super skinny with long legs and arms, plus I loved to climb everything. I'd do this thing where I'd hide and jump out at her. Once I sat on the top shelf of her bedroom closet for two hours waiting for her to get home from a play date. She opened the door and—*boom*—I popped down and landed right at her feet." I remember Cate's angry face and how she chased me out of her room. "She said I looked like a spider. The next morning, she called me Spider to make me mad, but I liked it, and it just kinda stuck." I pause, staring down at our hands. "She died when we were thirteen."

Her face falls. "God, I'm so sorry. What happened?"

"It's not something I talk about."

She nods, her face earnest. "I shouldn't have asked. I'm sorry."

I nod and look away. There's no way in hell I can tell her the truth—that I'm the reason my sister is gone.

AFTER TALKING ABOUT MOVIES AND books for almost two hours, Rose drifts off to sleep around hour three of the flight. I'm disappointed to not have her attention, but I know she's tired from her late night and then being scared of flying. As for me, I'm antsy the closer we get to Dallas and my father. I need a hit of something . . . anything.

Heidi walks by a few times, her eyes eating me up like I'm her last meal. I mostly ignore her, except to order a double shot of tequila. She's like the usual girls I see at shows . . . flirty and ready for anything. I fuck a lot of them. It's what I do.

But Rose . . . she's different.

Heidi returns with my drink and then leans down and whispers in my ear, "Wanna meet me in the bathroom at the back of the plane? You go in first, and I'll follow."

My gut says *hell no, don't do it,* but my brain . . . it needs something to shut it up.

She straightens up and bats her lashes at me. "Five minutes?"

I flick my eyes down to Rose and pause for a second, but then I turn back to Heidi and give her a short nod.

Fifteen minutes later, I'm feeling warm from the alcohol, but I still haven't left my seat.

Heidi walks by me again and sends me a lingering look. *Fuck me, please,* her eyes say.

I don't want her, not really. I want oblivion, yes, but that's different.

I want to stay right here with Rose.

And that's a huge fucking mistake.

Rule #1: Don't get your heart involved.

Why bother when people always leave anyway?

And with that thought in mind, I unbuckle and walk to the back.

I ease into the cramped, antiseptic-smelling bathroom and open the skull face on my sterling silver ring, revealing the white powder inside. I tap out a bump on the side of my hand and sniff it, the burn hitting me hard.

Yeah.

That's it.

Mixed with the tequila . . . *everything's gonna be okay.*

I hear the knock at the door and open it. She slithers in, smelling like a perfume counter at the mall and nothing like honey and vanilla. I don't let our eyes meet, and I don't kiss her on the mouth. But something doesn't feel right.

She must sense my hesitation because she unsnaps my jeans in a rush, whispering where to put my arms and legs to maximize the space. It only takes six minutes, tops, both of us reaching a new kind of high at thirty thousand feet. It fills my emptiness for a few moments, makes me forget there's a nice girl out there sitting in the seat next to mine, and for a moment, I almost let her in.

I finish and walk out of the toilet. She follows.

I won't recall her name. I never want to.

FIVE

Rose

THE FLIGHT ATTENDANT FLOUNCES PAST me with a gloating expression on her face, and I'm ready to pluck every hair out of her head. My hands clench around my seat.

How could he be with her? After kissing me?

Maybe I'm wrong.

Maybe they just went to talk.

Yeah right, Rose. Don't be an idiot.

An image of him with her dances around in my head as anger churns in my gut.

"Morning, sleepyhead," he calls out exuberantly as he slides back into his seat and buckles back up. "Looks like we're about to descend." I notice there's a flush to his face as he drums his fingers on his knees erratically. "You missed the fellow in 13B who snored so loud I thought I might have to stuff a sock down his throat. Crazy."

"Uh-huh."

"Are you okay?" he asks, spearing me with a look before

dropping my gaze.

I narrow my eyes, studying him. "Are you?"

His eyes bounce back to mine. "I'm fine. More than fine. I'm stoked and ready to deal with Dallas."

I don't know what that means, and I don't ask. I'm too mad to care what he's going to be doing in Dallas. I hope I never see him again.

"How was Heidi?" I say, keeping my face carefully composed even though I want to smack him.

He pales and opens his mouth to say something, but then compresses his lips and looks down at his hands. His index finger traces the lines of the LOST tattoo.

"Did you really have sex with her?" I was holding out hope that I was wrong.

He nods.

Disappointment slams into my chest, hurting more than it should have for a guy that I just met. "You're an asshole."

He swallows, talking fast. "I know, but nothing was going to happen between us. You're too nice for me and obviously we'll never see each other again, and trust me, if we had hooked up, I wouldn't have called you the next day and asked you out on a date. I don't do that—ever."

"No need to explain to me. I'm *not* jealous," I snap. "I feel sorry for you." I shove his jacket at him.

He puts it on slowly, his eyes still studying me, and even though I refuse to look back, my entire body feels the intensity of his gaze, as if I were under a microscope.

"Rose, look, it didn't mean anything. Sex never means any-thing with me."

"Nice to know you're such a slut." I ball my fists up.

Why did I let him affect me like this?

Because you'd liked him.

In the periphery of my gaze, I see him rub his face, his hands scrubbing at the dark shadow on his face.

"I didn't even kiss her—I don't *ever* kiss them." He doesn't say the words to my face, but rather at the seat in front of him.

I ignore him and stare out the window.

The plane begins its descent. Normally I'd be clinging to the seat, my heart in my throat, but I'm too revved up.

"I always screw shit up," he mutters.

We come to a halt on the landing strip and he shoots up as soon as we can, making his way to Heidi, who hands him his guitar and a piece of paper.

Probably with her phone number on it.

I hate to break it to her, but he won't be calling.

He sends a look back over his shoulder at me and my eyes blaze at him, even as my throat tightens.

I feel stupid.

Naïve.

At the exit, he turns around one more time, and his eyes meet mine as he tosses a tentative hand up as if to say goodbye.

I give him a one-finger salute.

He disappears from my view just as my phone buzzes with a text from Anne.

Robert and I are waiting for you downstairs next to baggage claim. We have a surprise for you. ☺ Love you bunches! Anne

Pushing down my anger at Spider, I groan. I hate Anne's surprises. Last year it was a drive to Tin Town to see my old house and neighborhood. She said it was because she wanted me to see how far I've come, but mostly I just felt sick, remembering Lyle and Mama. I hate Tin Town and what it took from me, yet it's who I am, and somehow I don't think I can ever outrun that.

What's going on? I respond.

You get to meet your new stepbrother today.

Oh. I frown, already in a shit mood. I can't recall Anne even telling me Robert Wainwright *had* a son.

But then I didn't know much about Robert at all. He and Anne are newly married and just back from their honeymoon.

Another text comes in but I don't check it because I'm too busy exiting the plane. I make a stop at the restroom to freshen up and change clothes before Anne sees me in this dress, which I know she won't approve of. I'm not a people pleaser, but I do try to keep things easy between us. How could I not? For the past four and a half years, she's taken care of me. She took me out of a foster system that was doing me no favors. In fact, the last home I lived in before Anne, I had to fight to keep one of the older boys from crawling in my bed at night. I was later removed from that house for kicking his teeth in. Trust me, Anne has her quirks, but without her, I never would have gotten to go to a private school or have nice clothes.

She wants a perfect little Highland Park girl and I do my best.

Except for secretly applying to NYU.

And getting my butterfly tattoo in New York.

Feeling excited, I look in the mirror and tug down the back of my dress at my neck to see how it's doing. Still red and sore, the hand-sized butterfly sits about three inches below my nape, and I know Anne is eventually going to see it, but I don't care. I'm in love with it because it reminds me of the beautiful boy who came into my life briefly when I was eleven. He flitted in and gave me hope. His kindness meant something and seeing it is a reminder.

Inside a stall, I take off my dress and slip on a pair of brown leggings and a modest, high-neck, maroon-colored sweater Anne bought for me. I pull out a pair of taupe booties and push them on my feet. After I dress, I remove the red lipstick and apply pink instead. I brush on a light coat of mascara, powder the sheen off my nose, and brush out my long hair until it shines.

After stuffing the dress and Converse into my backpack, I make my way to baggage claim, craning my neck to find Anne's blonde hair.

Because Robert is tall and dressed conspicuously in an expensive suit, I find him immediately and see Anne behind him. Dressed conservatively in a knee-length pencil skirt and heels with impeccable makeup, she has her attention on Robert and the person he's talking to—a tall guy in a gray leather jacket.

Whatttt?

I stop breathing as realization dawns.

Robert's English. Spider's English.

No.

No way in hell.

My eyes bounce back and forth between Robert and Spider as they stand there talking.

They're *nothing* alike.

They're like night and day, fire and ice.

Maybe they're just chatting, old buddies who realized they were from the same country.

My phone pings again and I pull it out to see two texts from Anne. The first one was sent while I was still on the plane but was too busy to get.

Your stepbrother was on the plane.

And there it is . . . confirmed.

The next one is **Where are you?**

She must have just sent it.

I look back up to watch as Anne turns to Spider and hugs him. It doesn't take a person like me who reads others well to see that she's uncomfortable with him right away. The truth is in her stiff countenance and the way she keeps throwing glances Robert's way. Robert moves to stand next to her as both of them talk to Spider. I don't miss that his dad's eyes are narrowed on him, raking over him, as if searching for something.

Spider hasn't seen me yet, and I watch as he pushes back hair that has fallen into his face, tugging on the ends as if he's anxious. I notice the vulnerable look to his shoulders as he slumps down to fiddle with his guitar. A small part of me forgets my anger and wonders what's going on with him and his dad.

I cling to my pillow and pretend it's a wall between Spider and myself as I march over to where they stand. My heart pounds so hard I'm sure everyone in the vicinity can hear it. I'm nervous and angry yet strangely excited about seeing Spider again.

"Clarence has been on the road for the past few months," Robert's telling Anne as I approach.

"Can't you call me Spider like everyone else?" Spider says, a tightness to his face.

Robert ignores him, his eyes going over Spider's shoulder to me. He motions for him to be quiet. "Hang on, there's Rose," I hear him say.

Anne waves and then grabs my hand as I reach them. She pulls me in for a light cheek kiss, the scent of her perfume familiar and comforting even though we aren't terribly close. I smile broadly at her as she asks how I am and how the flight was. I reply normally. No way am I going to let on anything about Spider. I can already sense that things are iffy between him and his dad, and no matter his faults, I don't want to add to their particular family drama.

I watch out of my peripheral vision as Spider slowly turns to face me.

Surprise is on his face, more so as his eyes take in the change of clothing and the subdued lipstick.

Robert, who I only met a few months ago when Anne announced she was pregnant, smiles at me. We're still feeling each other out, but my initial impression of him is that he's a lot like Anne . . . conservative and a bit unemotional.

He gestures to Spider. "Clarence, I'd like for you to meet Rose, your new stepsister."

Spider grasps my hand, and a current zips between us. I recall that kiss on the plane even though I don't want to.

Both of us just stand there.

I think he's reeling.

I know I am.

I tug my hand away, realizing we've been holding hands too long for it to be normal.

"She's seventeen," Robert says carefully in his clipped tones, his eyes going from me to Spider.

A flash of surprise crosses Spider's face before he quickly covers it. "Is that right? I thought you were . . . older," he says, a bit of an accusation in his tone.

My lips flatten and I nod. "It's because I'm tall, but one should never assume. How old are you?"

"Twenty-two. It feels like I was seventeen a million years ago."

"It's nice to meet you," I say because I don't know what else to say. This is the weirdest situation I've ever found myself in—and that's saying a lot. My stepbrother is a guy I kissed on the

plane . . . who later screwed the flight attendant. There's no etiquette book for that.

"Did you see each other on the plane?" Robert asks.

My lips tighten. "I didn't see him." Which was true. I saw a
guy I built up in my head, a guy who was sweet and kissed me
like he meant it.

I didn't know this other person.

Robert looks at Spider, who's currently gazing at me, a look
of regret on his face.

That look . . . it makes me falter for a moment, but I rally
back. I'm not letting him get to me again.

"I look forward to getting to know you," he says, his eyes on
my face, as if he's trying to figure me out. Then, in front of God
and everyone at the airport, he leans down and lightly brushes my
cheek with his lips. His touch makes my body hum and my heart
flip-flop. *Stupid, stupid heart.*

AFTER A RATHER STILTED DRIVE in Robert's black Mercedes,
during which Spider keeps darting looks at me, we finally arrive at
Robert and Anne's house in Highland Park. Robert has lived here
for several years, at least when he isn't traveling around the globe to
manage his real estate company, and Anne recently moved in with
him. I have a bedroom here, but I've only stayed over a few times.
I prefer Anne's last house, which is also in a great neighborhood,
but much smaller than this one. She sold it as soon as they married.

Once Robert parks the car in the circle drive, I can't get out
fast enough. I need some space from Spider.

Instead of going inside the house, I hug Anne and Robert

outside the front door with a promise to show up for dinner later that evening. Anne wants me to come in and tell her more about New York, but I tell her I'm tired. She seems to understand.

As I'm walking to my Highlander that I parked here while I was gone, Spider calls out to me. I turn and watch him stalk toward me.

"Yeah? What is it?" I say sharply as I toss my backpack in the car, ready to get away and process all the crazy stuff that's happened today.

He shifts from one foot to the next. "I-I just wanted to say that I'm sorry. Again."

I stiffen, needing more than just an apology from him, but I don't know what that is. The level of emotion he brings out in me surprises me. "It doesn't matter. It's over and done. Now we have to get along." My lips twist. "Like you said, nothing was going to happen between us anyway, right?"

"Right. Especially since you're *underage.*" He emphasizes the last word and I flush.

"You have no right to judge," I say.

He sticks his hands in his pockets and grimaces. "I know. You have every right to hate me."

"I don't hate you. I could never hate you."

I don't know why that's true with him, but it is. Maybe it's because I can sense there's more under the surface with him. He's got issues, and I can relate to that with my background. I glance over his shoulder to see Robert is still at the door, watching us with a contemplative look on his face.

My anger eases more as I move my eyes from his dad to him. I suspect something awful happened between those two. "What's up with your dad?"

I don't miss that Spider's shoulders square as if he's preparing for battle. "We don't get along."

"Then why are you here?"

He pauses. "I haven't seen him in six months, and he wanted me to clock in and meet the *new* family. So, here I am." He holds his hands out and smirks.

There's more to this story, but I don't push it. Yet.

He tosses a look over his shoulder at Robert and I see an almost imperceptible nod he gives him as if saying, *I see you and I'm coming.*

"See you later, Rose."

He sends me one final look and then he's striding down the driveway toward the house.

I watch until he's at the door with Robert, taking in the good two feet of space they keep between their bodies, a telltale sign of tension. I notice that Robert's face is more somber than usual, as if Spider has done something he disapproves of.

I file it all away and plan to figure it out later.

Right now, I'm ready to get out of here, so I hop in my car and hightail it back to the dorms at Claremont, about ten minutes away.

On the drive over, I focus on the next few weeks and the studying I need to do before graduation. I'm in all honors classes, and I do my best to stay at the top. Granny is always on my mind, and it encourages me to think about how proud she'd be that I'm going to make something of myself.

A staccato knock hits my door after an hour of being back, and I fling open the door to see my two best friends. Dressed in a leather skirt and an off-the-shoulder denim blouse, Lexa enters the room like she owns the place. We've been inseparable since freshman year when we both ended up in the same horrible tennis class where neither of us could hit a decent volley. Like me, she lives in student housing since her family lives in Atlanta. Unlike me, she was brought up with a silver spoon in her mouth, but she's nice anyway.

Her mouth widens. "Oh my God, I'm so freaking glad you're back! This dump has been D-E-A-D for spring break. I didn't have anyone to talk to!"

"You had me, but apparently I'm not good enough!" Oscar says offhandedly as he flies in the door right behind her, rather dramatically, the long coattails from his black leather duster flapping. His mop of brown curls bobs as he grabs me and air-kisses both of my cheeks. "God, I've missed you. By the way, Lexa is a little bitch when you aren't here to keep her sane. How was New York? Did you see any models? Actors? Anyone? God, this city sucks. Let's move to New York and live in a loft together—like on *Friends*."

I giggle at his barrage of questions.

A scholarship student from a small rural town outside of Dallas, he's my oldest friend at Claremont Prep. In fact, we met the moment I walked in the office on my first day to pick up my schedule. He took one look at my no doubt terrified face and immediately offered to show me around campus. We bonded over our love for fashion and great literature. I don't know what I'd do without him. He's my tribe, and our dream is to live together in New York.

Oscar grins. "Did you fall in love with the campus? Does Anne know how bad you want to move? Will she let you leave the state of Texas?"

Lexa opens her compact and reapplies her already perfect lipstick. "We all know the answer to that one—*no*. Anne wants you right here so she can show you off as the girl she saved from the streets. You're her little prize."

"That's mean," Oscar says as he throws a pillow at her. "I'm taking Lexa off our prayer list, Rose."

I shake my head and grin. "What prayer list?"

He lifts his hands. "The one I'm going to start for all the people who need prayers around here."

I giggle. Man, I missed him.

Lexa ignores Oscar, still focusing on Anne. "She *literally* made you the poster girl at her charity gala last year when she put you *on a poster*. You gave a speech about the inner city and everything. She's molding you to be a mini-Anne. You already dress how she wants." She waves her hands at my outfit.

I grimace at Lexa's words. I'm not a mini-Anne. I'm just *me*. Yes, Anne likes to take me to her charity events and show me off because I'm a success story, but she also pays for me to take self-defense classes because it makes me feel more secure. I owe her.

I look at Lexa, taking in the expensive clothes and the Louis Vuitton she casually tossed on my bed when she arrived. She doesn't get it because she's never had to worry about where her next meal might come from. *I have.* "Some of those kids come from horrible situations, and if I can be a reason someone contributes . . . then I'll do my part."

Her face softens as she looks at me. "Gah, I am so sorry. You must think I'm an awful person. Of course, you want to help those kids. It's who you are." She waves her hands. "I'm just anxious for you because I know how much you want to go to NYU—and she isn't going to let you."

I bite my lip. I don't want to think about that right now.

Oscar tosses a long arm around my shoulder and squeezes. "Ignore Lexa—she's on her period. Just tell us all the juicy bits about your trip."

So I do. I tell them about Spider—from the club last night, to the kiss, to the flight attendant, and then the stepbrother bomb.

There is a brief, wide-eyed silence before Oscar explodes. "You kissed a random dude on a *plane*? How did you not barf on him? I thought you hated flying?"

"I do."

He spins in a circle, clearly excited. "Oh my God, you like your stepbrother. It's so . . . *twisted*." He rubs his hands together. "It's like that movie *Clueless* where the heroine has the hots for her stepbrother. I love it."

"I don't like him," I declare, but it feels wrong to say that, and I inhale a deep breath. "And have you forgotten the part where he screws the girl in the bathroom? You should be angry with him on my behalf."

"True . . . and I am." He pulls out his phone. "But right now, I gotta see this guy for myself."

"And you're going to see him tonight at dinner?" Lexa asks. "Maybe you can use your appetizer fork to poke his eyeballs out." Her heavily lashed eyes are dead serious.

"You're scary," Oscar comments as he scrolls on his phone.

She thinks about it, a little glint in her gaze. "But seriously . . . here's an idea: maybe you should go after this bad boy and then pull a whammy on him and break his heart." She nods. "Yeah, I like that much better. Less blood and guts on the dinner plate."

"Hmmm, maybe." The idea does intrigue me. "I don't think he has a heart to break though."

Oscar holds up a triumphant pic of him along with members of his band, who I recognize from the show at the bar. "Holy shit, Sherlock, this dude's gorgeous." He scrolls down. "I'm on the band's Facebook page, and let me tell ya, he is sex-ay."

Lexa smirks. "Stop saying *sex-ay*. You're not going to make it a thing, not here at Claremont, not in Dallas, and not in New York."

He flips her off, and she giggles.

I look at Oscar. "Speaking of New York . . . did you hear back about your scholarship to NYU?"

"I've been accepted, of course, but I don't know about the scholarship . . ." His voice trails off, and I hear the worry there. He's at Claremont on a full ride because he's super smart, but NYU rarely gives full rides, and without the financial aid the scholarship would provide—he can't go. He should have heard something by now, and I'm holding out that he gets one.

He plucks at a string on his jacket. "I can always go to UT. They'll take me." His voice is uncharacteristically subdued.

I exhale, taking in his pensive face. He wants out of Texas as much as I do. I'm running to get away from my past, and he's running from a dysfunctional family that looks down on him for being gay.

"We'll get there . . . together," I say to him. "Somehow."

Oscar shrugs and I can tell he doesn't want to talk about it. He looks at the picture of Spider again. "I can't believe you locked lips with this piece of deliciousness. Did you die?"

I shake my head at him and laugh. "No. I'm quite alive."

I can't help but lean over and study the group photo and get a peek inside Spider's life. In the picture, he's standing in the middle of his friends on a beach with a drink up in the air as if he's toasting. Wearing a Union Jack hat and a pair of athletic shorts, he's shirtless, his broad chest tan and muscled. He looks hot. It reminds me of him stalking around the stage in his mink coat. Unbidden, a small smile grows on my face. Something about him . . . even though I'm angry with him . . . calls to me.

I ignore it and forge on.

"He likes to be the center of everything," I say.

"He can get in my center any time," Lexa chimes in as she leans over my shoulder.

Oscar cocks his head, not looking too sure. "If you do decide to break his heart like Lexa said, you better be careful with this one. Those eyes . . ."

Tell me about it.

Lexa snorts. "You just want him for yourself."

"I want everyone, sweetie." He tosses his scarf around his neck and poses.

I laugh as I get up and open my closet. "I'm the one who has to have dinner with him tonight."

Oscar jumps and peers inside, rummaging through the hangers. "If you're seeing the hottie, then wear this!" He pulls out a silky red dress, one he and I found at a secondhand store downtown. With spaghetti straps and a keyhole in the back, it's short and flirty and not Anne approved. I adore it. "It's cut up to your butt crack and he won't be able to stop looking at those long legs of yours. Pair it with those silver knock-off Jimmy Choos I found." He kisses his fingertips. "Perfection."

"I'm wearing my hair in a ponytail, old jeans, and flip-flops. I'm not even going to brush my hair, or my teeth." I'm teasing, of course, but I love to see their faces.

Lexa giggles. "Anne will die."

Oscar's face is theatrically devastated. "Please, Rose. He's a potential rock star. Impress him, then break his heart."

"Nope."

Lexa ignores my comment and rises up from the bed where she plopped down earlier and begins rummaging through my underwear drawer. "You need a thong for that dress."

I laugh. "I'm not wearing that stupid dress to dinner. That's enough from both of you. I need to finish up this assignment before Monday, plus I have a paper to work on."

They grumble but comply. Lexa mutters something about hitting the mall, and Oscar says he has plans to see a movie. Eventually, I get them out the door and focus back on my studies, but every few minutes, I sneak a look over at the red dress Oscar hung on the outside of my closet.

A little spike of excitement goes through me as I imagine Spider seeing me in it.

But then there's Anne. She won't like it.

A small part of me doesn't care. Maybe it's because of the *mini-Anne* comment or maybe it's because I know that Spider is attracted to me and I want him to suffer as I sit across from him at dinner.

Yes, a little voice whispers in my head. *Wear it. Mess with the bad boy.*

SIX

Spider

"THE FIRST RULE OF THIS house is you cannot, I repeat, you *cannot* fool around with Rose." Waving his hands around, he continues, "We all know about your . . . reputation with women, but she's your stepsister and has a bright future ahead of her." My father's tone is sharp as nails as I sit across from him in a hard chair in his study. We came in here as soon as we arrived from the airport.

Rose. I blow out a breath as regret eats at me over what happened on the plane.

No doubt he saw the way I looked at her.

"I saw how you were looking at her. She's too young for you, so don't get any ideas."

I raise a brow. "I'm not getting ideas." But I'm lying to him. Rose fascinates me. She's beautiful and sweet—

I cut those thoughts off.

She's done with me, and I don't blame her one bit.

She *should* be angry with me. She doesn't deserve someone as fucked up as I am.

I stuff thoughts of her in a box, put a chain around it, and toss it in a dark corner of my mind.

I'll forget about her, I tell myself.

After all, pushing people away is something I learned well from my father.

Tall and imposing with broad shoulders and a face made of granite, he's a man who slams doors, speaks curtly, and gets shit done—no matter the cost.

He's nothing like Mum, who is sunshine and light, but then at least he stuck around a little. Six months after Cate died, she was out the door with a new lover in tow. I still see her from time to time, in between boyfriends and vacations in exotic places. Our relationship is . . . sticky. I think it's hard for her to see me and not think of Cate. On the other hand, it's hard for me to see Mum and not think of her leaving me.

Father's voice brings me back to the present. "Secondly, no drugs around Anne and Rose. It won't be tolerated."

My eyes find his and I exhale, my fingers twitchy as I drum them on my jeans. "With all these rules, I'm surprised you even invited me."

He lets out a deep breath. "Believe it or not, I want you to be part of my new family. We haven't seen each other in months."

My lips tighten. "Six to be precise."

Which is not unusual. When we first moved to the US, I barely saw him at all. He tucked me away in an exclusive boarding school called Briarwood and pretended I didn't exist. I was a mixed up thirteen-year-old kid then, fresh from Cate dying and Mum leaving, yet he went on about his life as if nothing had happened.

I'm sure he sees that entire part of our lives differently, but I don't. He deserted me when I needed him the most.

He gets up and pours himself a Scotch and sits back down at his desk. "Look, I just want you to hang around Dallas for a few days and get to know Anne. I also want to make sure you're . . . okay. I hope you're clean, Clarence. You don't want to go back to rehab."

My hands clench, remembering the two months I spent at a "spa" in Northern California a few years ago. "I don't have a drug problem. I've never been better." Lies. All lies. But I don't care. I'm irritable and crashing from before, and I just want to end this conversation. I need a fucking bump. My fingers rub my ring. Maybe I can sneak off to one of the bathrooms upstairs . . .

I refocus as I feel Father studying me, searching for signs of me using. "I'm fine," I say, my tone sharp.

He swallows and nods his head. "Okay. You're welcome to stay here or at the penthouse I have in the city."

I nod. "I'll take the penthouse."

"Fine," he says, and I don't miss the look of relief on his face. The thing is, he probably does want me here to meet his new wife and to check on me, but I do make him uncomfortable. Staying at the penthouse is easier on everyone.

I clear my throat. "You mentioned a monetary gift? An early inheritance, perhaps?" When he called to invite me, he said he'd make it worth my time, and I assumed that's what he meant. I study him, searching for answers.

"Of course." He takes a drag from his Scotch, and I eye it enviously.

I fold my hands in my lap. "How much money are we talking?"

He's never given me anything. I'm not a trust fund baby. Sure, he paid for my boarding school and expenses, but once he figured out I wasn't going to college, my Amex card was canceled. I've been supporting myself for the past five years. He called it tough love; I called it an arsehole who wanted to control my life. Maybe he's right—maybe I should get a degree—but music is what I crave. It's my skin, my fucking everything. I can't breathe without it.

He taps a pen on the mahogany desk. "You mentioned moving to LA with the band. I imagine the expenses are high there if you want to fit in with the right crowd. I'll do a hundred thousand."

Holy shit. I try to keep the surprise from showing on my face. I expected maybe ten or twenty if he was feeling magnanimous. Frankly, I'm surprised he's even offering me anything. I mean, I would have come anyway . . . eventually. He's my father, and I still crave his approval after all these years.

Is it possible he's trying to make amends?

He sighs and leans back in his leather chair, a tired expression flitting across his face. Lines feather out from his eyes, and I see that his hair has thinned considerably since the last time I saw him.

"You're fifty-five this month?" I ask.

"I'm surprised you remembered." He glances past me to look out the window at the carefully manicured grounds of the house, and I follow his eyes and see Anne sitting on one of the benches in the garden. She's his type, namely beautiful and younger than him, maybe in her early forties. But, I'm surprised he's remarried.

"After Mum left, I figured you'd written off marriage for good."

In the years they've been apart, I've never known him to have a serious relationship longer than a few months, just a long line of pretty girlfriends who came and went.

"It's different this time with Anne." He rubs at a wrinkle on the bridge of his nose.

"Migraine?" I ask. He gets them nearly every time he sees

me—just part of my charm.

"No." He sighs heavily.

"Then what gives?"

There are a few beats of silence, the tension in the room shifting from me to him as his gaze drifts back over to his wife. His countenance softens. "She's pregnant."

"Shit." My mouth flaps open. "How? Why didn't you tell me that right off the bat?"

He laughs, the first one since he's been with me. "I don't know. I'm still . . . reeling from it. We met at a hotel convention and I thought I'd never see her again, but then she called me with the news." An incredulous smile flashes across his face. "She's five months along. It's like . . . I'm starting all over again."

I'm reeling too. "Haven't you ever heard of a condom?"

"Indeed." He gets up from his seat and paces around the darkly paneled room. "Anne is just as shocked as I am. She was told she'd never have kids." He pauses. "She adopted Rose four years ago."

Ah, interesting. I noticed they don't favor at all.

"Anne never married?" I ask.

"No. She tried several IVF attempts with a donor, but nothing worked." An uncharacteristic look of uncertainty crosses his face. "We've already had some complications with the pregnancy, and things have been touch and go. It's important that you be on your best behavior around Anne. I was a bit hesitant at first, but now . . . I find that I'm quite happy."

I start, coming to attention.

Quite happy?

Bollocks! That's as good as a declaration of love from Father. It's huge.

I pick at the frayed hole in my jeans. "So, you're going to be a good father?" *Because you weren't with me* is implied and he knows it.

Smoke-colored eyes land on mine, and I see something there . . . perhaps regret. "I want to be."

I tap my fingers against my chair, ready to get out of here and process everything. It's been a crazy as hell day . . . a seventeen-year-old stepsister I want to fuck, a new stepmother who disapproves of me already (I can tell), and now a new baby.

I change the topic, heading back to the crux of the matter. I steeple my fingers and give him a long look. Being on my own has taught me to go for what I want. "Back to the money . . . I'll do everything you ask of me for two hundred thousand."

His eyes flare, and I see a hint of admiration in them. "You making a deal with me?"

I nod. "And you have to call me Spider. No more of this Clarence bullshit. Cate gave me the name, and it's mine. It's something you can't take away from me."

He takes another swig of his Scotch, his eyes lingering on mine before drifting out to rest on Anne. He gazes back at me and nods, signaling that our meeting is over. "Deal."

SEVEN

Rose

THIS ENTIRE DAY HAS BEEN bizarre and sucked the wind right out of me. The only way to get pumped back up is to crank "Defying Gravity" and sing it as loud as I can as I drive out to Highland Park. It's my favorite song in the musical *Wicked* mostly because it's about empowerment, about leaping into the unknown as you trust your instincts and push ahead with what you think is right. I *want* to be that girl. Desperately. I want to take a leap and be everything I ever imagined . . .

But not in Highland Park.

With a sigh, I whip through the double gates and park alongside Robert's Mercedes.

Anne and I had lived comfortably in a Dallas suburb, but this house is insane. It's a three-story whitewashed brick with French country details, from the rustic shutters on the tall windows to the huge medieval-looking front door. Around the back is a covered patio with two fireplaces, a mountain lake-shaped pool, and an outdoor kitchen that looks like it belongs in a magazine. Beyond the pool is an intricate garden, complete with a little maze of shrubs, stone benches, and alcoves. Sitting on about five acres, the estate is one of the biggest in Highland Park.

I try to picture Spider growing up here, but I can't. He doesn't fit in here, and neither do I.

I ring the doorbell because this doesn't feel like home to me, and a freshly showered Spider answers, looking infuriatingly handsome with damp hair and wearing a a pair of low-slung jeans with a black Beatles tee. My traitorous eyes linger on his well-defined shoulders.

A small smile toys around his lips. "Hello, Miss Seventeen." His accent washes over me, clipped, soft, and deep with layers.

And just like that, I'm under his spell, sucked into his allure all over again. I recall our kiss . . . the magic of it . . . the way his hands cupped my face.

Feeling frustrated, I stuff those thoughts and feelings down and brush past him into the foyer. "Let's get one thing straight, *stepbrother*, your sexy little accent won't work on me."

"I never said it would, *stepsister*." He leans against the wall, his copper eyes drifting lazily over my outfit. His lip twitches. "Did you wear that for my benefit?"

I straighten my shoulders, my body automatically remembering the deportment lessons I took. Yes, I wore the red dress and heels. And I look good.

I glide past him, like a gazelle . . . maybe. "I wore it for me." Lie.

"I'm not surprised. I'm not worth dressing up for. You look beautiful, by the way." He gets a pensive look on his face as he stares at me, and I sigh, reminding myself that he *is* my new stepbrother, and I do have to be an adult and get along with him. I brush my gaze over his attire. "No mesh tank top? I must confess, I'm going to miss all those tattoos on display."

He shoots me a quick look, as if trying to suss out if I'm teasing him or not. His eyes search mine, and I smile, just a little one. A gruff laugh comes out of him, and for the first time since the whole flight attendant thing, there's a slight easing between us.

I clear my throat and stick out my hand. "I'm hoping we can be friends. What do you think?"

He takes my hand as sparks fire over my skin. "Fine with me."

I arch a brow. "Pretending not to care is usually the tendency of someone who really does care the most . . . *Clarence*."

He tosses his head back and laughs, the sound clear and deep. It ignites a memory in me, one from my childhood. I grapple to hang on to it but it drifts away quickly.

Our hands part, a bit reluctantly, as his eyes gleam down at me. "You know, I hate that name with a passion, but hearing it on your lips . . . not so much."

"I'm serious. It's called a defense mechanism, and people do it so they won't get hurt."

He squints at me. "Anyone ever tell you that you read into things too much?"

"Maybe." I look down at my hands, noticing they are nervously twisting the straps on my small clutch. I have my own tells. "I do like to analyze people."

"And what did you figure out about me?" His eyes gaze into mine before he glances at himself in the mirror. It's as if he's afraid to look at me for too long, and I wonder why.

I infuse my voice with confidence I don't actually have. "That you're dangerous."

"Me? Why?"

I chew on my bottom lip. "You don't care who you hurt to avoid feeling anything, which probably means you've been hurt in the past. You have demons."

He freezes, his gaze coming back to my face. "Looks like you got me pegged then."

I hesitate. "We all have demons, right? In some form or another."

He just stares at me. "What's your demon, Rose?"

"I don't belong here. It's like I'm playing a game of pretend." I glance around the grand house. "This isn't the kind of home I'm used to. It's the same when I'm at Claremont. I don't fit in with those kids. I grew up in Tin Town, probably not what you would have expected."

He watches me as I talk—or more like *ramble*—making me nervous.

"I never fit in either when I was at prep school." He pauses. "You aren't anything like I expected. When Robert mentioned a younger stepsister on the phone, I pictured a little girl in pigtails and a school uniform."

"I do have a school uniform."

A serious expression appears on his face. "You know, I never would have kissed you if I'd known your true age. I know better than that."

I stiffen, feeling defensive. I recall the hell I grew up with, the foster homes, the times I had to fight to defend my virtue. "I may be seventeen, but I'm not a kid."

Robert appears in the foyer, his eyes bouncing from me to Spider, his gaze searching.

"Everything okay out here?"

I nod as Spider clams up and brushes past us to head into the formal living room.

It's a spacious affair with a beamed ceiling and a fireplace framed by whitewashed stone. The focal point of the room is the pair of charcoal drawings that hang on the wall behind the cream leather sectional.

Spider blinks as he walks around the coffee table and stands in front of the pictures. My interest piqued, I follow him while Robert moves to make himself a drink at the bar. I stand next to Spider, our shoulders not quite touching as we look at the art.

The one on the right is a Tudor-style home made of stone with intricate dormers and arched doors. The other one is a little boy lying spread-eagle on the grass as he stares up at the sky with a big grin on his face. It's perfectly mischievous.

I study them both closely, taking in the childlike quality to the art. I think I see his name scrawled in the corner of one of the drawings. "Yours?"

He nods, indicating the drawing on the right. "Just the one of the house. The other was drawn by my sister Cate."

A ghost of a smile flits across Spider's mouth. "We both loved to draw, but she was always better about capturing people."

His fingers are magic with a guitar, so it's not surprising that he can draw as well. "They're both very good." I motion toward the little boy. "I bet you were a handful."

"I had the attention span of a gnat." A long sigh comes from him. "I was her favorite subject. She meant . . . a lot to me." Darkness crosses his face, and I immediately want to make it go away.

"Is that where you grew up?" I tilt my head at the house.

He nods. "That was our family estate, my real home, and we had the run of it. Mum and Father were gone a lot, but with Cate around, there was always something to do." He tucks his hands in his pockets. "It's been a while since I've seen these. I-I didn't even know he'd put them up."

"Why did you leave London?" He alluded to it earlier on the plane with his *fresh start* comment, but I'm curious for more.

"Father . . . he wanted away from the memories."

"What memories?"

His eyes turn to me, and you know the saying that eyes are the windows to the soul? I read his. Spider's luminous amber eyes enrapture me, capturing me with their loneliness.

My breath hitches.

He opens his mouth to say something more but Robert's voice comes from across the room, interrupting our conversation. "Rose, tell me about your classes this semester. How's it going?" There's a sharp quality in his voice, and I turn over my shoulder to watch him as he crosses the room toward us, his carefully creased slacks moving with each step.

I frown. He clearly cares about Anne, and I like him a lot, mostly because he softens Anne and makes her happy, giving me more space. But it's clear he doesn't want Spider to be around me. I noticed it earlier at the door when he watched us—and now he's trying to interrupt our obviously private conversation.

As if Spider senses the tension in the air, he steps away from me and sits down on the couch.

He'll learn that I don't give up that easy. Something about him makes me want to dig for more. I want his story.

I'm saved from further talking as Anne waltzes into the room looking lovely in a pink flowy ankle-length maxi dress that artfully conceals her growing belly.

She runs her eyes over my red dress, pausing on the hemline, a small wrinkle forming on her forehead. "I don't think I've ever seen you wear that."

It's her way of saying I look awful.

Feeling self-conscious, I touch the bodice of the silk garment. "It's something Oscar found for me at one of his consignment stores. It's vintage, I think. I like it." I fidget, feeling uncomfortable as her scowl grows. She runs her eyes over my hair and I'm glad I wore it down since it covers the tattoo.

"I don't," she says.

Robert tosses an arm around Anne. "She looks beautiful, dear. Don't give her a hard time."

Anne's lips tighten and I'm not surprised. I expected her disapproval and wore it anyway. I rarely rebel against her, but lately with the whole NYU thing, I feel antsy.

She exhales. "The next time you come, dress more modestly. That dress is too short and gives off the wrong impression." She smiles brightly at me like she usually does after a criticism. I call it her "cut and hug" routine. She turns to Robert, not waiting for my reply. "Now, how about a soda?"

"Bloody hell, they're rather scary," Spider whispers from behind me as Robert and Anne walk over to the bar so he can make her a ginger ale.

"What do you mean?" I ask, turning to face him.

He palms his spider tattoo. "I mean, Father's acting weird, and Anne is . . . rather strict." He brushes his gaze over me, lingering on the bodice of my dress, and I get tingles. "Don't listen to her. I love the dress." He grins. "After all, you did wear it for me, right?"

I shake my head at him. He goes from deep to cocky in the space of a few minutes. I can't keep up with him.

"Anne's big on appearances. She doesn't want me turning into my mama, and her way of making sure that doesn't happen is to tell me every single move to make." I sigh.

"Don't let her squash your spirit." He searches my face. "If you ever want to talk, I'm here—as a stepbrother, of course."

I picture us talking . . . then kissing . . . then doing more. I imagine his hands on my body, slipping under my dress . . .

Shit. Where did that come from? I suck in a breath. *Forget those thoughts, Rose.*

I nod. "Right."

AFTER DINNER, SPIDER EXCUSES HIMSELF to go upstairs to his room. He mentioned he's staying at the penthouse but he's yet to head that way.

He barely said much during our five-course meal, his eyes fixed firmly on his plate. I don't like it that he's different around Robert and Anne. I want my snarky Englishman from the plane.

Twenty minutes later, he dashes down the stairs dressed in black gym shorts and an athletic shirt.

"Running?" I ask stupidly as he makes his way to the front door.

"Yeah. I need to get out of this place for a bit." With his hand on the doorknob, he glances back at me. "You wanna come?"

I send him a wry look. "My heels weren't made for running. I was thinking we might get Robert and Anne and play some games. Scrabble?"

"Scrabble? *My father?*" His face is surprised, and I can see that he's probably never played many games with Robert. Again, I wonder what's between them, and part of me, the part that's like Granny, wants to analyze their relationship and maybe help mend it. "It might be fun to get to know each other better."

He shakes his head and backs away. "I don't even know what fucking universe this is. I gotta go."

The door opens and he's gone, his tall form slipping out into the night.

I stand at the open door and watch him disappear as he jogs away.

WE PLAY A ROUND OF Scrabble, and by ten, Robert retires to give Anne and me some time alone.

As usual, our conversation is formal and very matter-of-fact. She's not a warm and fuzzy person.

"So, how was NYU?" Her voice has an undertone of concern.

"They have a great psychology department, and one of the professors I talked to is from Dallas. It would be like a little bit of home." I hold my breath. "I'd like to go to NYU."

She shakes her head. "I want you to stay close by. The baby will be here soon—don't you want to be here? I might need the help on the weekends."

She won't need my help. I've already overheard her and Robert discussing hiring a nanny. "I could come home for the holidays."

She sends me a look—you know the one, like I should have known the answer before I even asked. "It pains me to even hear you talk that way." She pats my leg. "Let's put a pin in the NYU thing for a while, okay? See how things go next year?"

She's patronizing me, and I stiffen. "I can always pay for it myself," I say. "I'm working three nights a week at Jo's." Jo's is a local diner where I've waited tables since last August. I like working because it makes me feel like I have a purpose. Anne didn't approve of my decision to work, but I'd insisted. She would have preferred for me to work at the country club or at one of the boutiques in town, but that wasn't me.

She frowns and rubs her belly. "That's ridiculous. You won't make NYU tuition money at the diner. Plus, you're too late to even apply for this year."

I exhale. Obviously, Robert and Anne have the money to send me to NYU—Winston is just as pricey—she just doesn't want me to go because she likes having me around to control. And because she's done so much for me already, I hate to ask her for anything she doesn't want to give me. Maybe the new baby will change her.

But still . . .

This NYU thing . . .

I can't let it go forever . . . but I can let it go for right now.

Anne's voice pulls me back. She's rising up from the couch, and I presume she's headed to bed. She walks over to me, her eyes searching. "Also, I noticed that you stared at Spider a lot during dinner. I want you to be polite to him, but he has a history of drug use, and, of course, he's into his music. You know what kind of lifestyle those types have."

I sigh, annoyed with her. Again. Sometimes it feels like Anne is the child and I'm the adult. "Spider's okay. I like him."

She arches her brows. "Just don't like him too much."

"Yes ma'am."

I don't tell her that it's too late.

EIGHT

Spider

RUN.

I run until I can't fucking breathe and my chest hurts.

Sweaty and tired, I stop in a nearby park with plenty of streetlights to catch my breath. My head is full of my father, his new wife, and Rose.

Everything inside me feels upside down from my crazy day. I scrub my face. Sometimes exercising keeps the cravings at bay, but right now, it's not working.

I need something hard to chase everything away.

Exhausted, I park my arse on a bench and make a plan for the evening. I could go back to the house for the night, but for some reason I'm scared and it has a lot to do with Rose. I need to stay away from her. Even though I barely know her, she's somehow managed to get under my skin.

I heave out a long exhale, feeling alone. They're back at the house laughing and playing Scrabble. They're a family, and I don't fit in.

I change directions and think about our band and how we've been on the road for the past several months, hitting bars and small music halls all over the US. We've done well to not have a record label. It's not crazy money, but it's enough to push us into finding a permanent residence in LA, somewhere to put down roots. Sebastian's from there and he knows a couple of record producers he wants to work with. He's the only family I really have . . .

Which brings me back to the Scrabble game.

Fuck. I really don't want to go back to that mansion. After some thinking, I decide to pick up my clothes and guitar tomorrow. I call an Uber to take me to The Galleria to shop for the basics: jeans, some random shirts, a pair of leather flip-flops, and underwear. After my shopping, I haul ass to the penthouse and shower.

An hour later, I'm sitting at a bar in Uptown. I order a shot of tequila just as a curvy brunette walks up to me. She reminds me of Rose with her long hair, but she has that rich girl vibe about her that I recognize from a mile away—petulant face, expensive purse, and bought boobs.

She says her name is Kirsten, and I buy her a drink. Hell, I buy her several drinks.

We sneak off to the bathroom and I pull her in a stall where we do a line together and she sucks me off. Later, I throw myself around on the dance floor to some techno music shit that I usually hate. I feel fucking amazing. Life is good. I can handle anything with a drink, a girl, and some coke.

An hour later, we're tossing back more drinks when she whispers in my ear, her hands rubbing down my chest. "My car's just outside and my condo is a mile from here. You wanna take this party there?"

I smile down at her.

I don't even pause. "Indeed."

She stands on her tiptoes to kiss me, but I avoid her lips with a quick turn of my face.

Rose pops into my head, with her wide green eyes and the way she *gets me*. She knows what a poser I am—that I have a fucking *defense mechanism* of all things.

I have to forget her.

"Let's leave," I say to the girl.

I pay the check, and we get in her white Lexus. She drives us, even though she's probably drunk. Streetlights flash by as I rest back against the leather interior.

"You from Dallas?" the girl asks me, and I realize we barely exchanged personal information past our names.

I grunt an affirmation, not wanting to talk to her. Dallas just reminds me that my father is starting all over with a new family when he was never *really* my family.

We park and I make it all the way to her door before I start getting hot, and not in a good way. I feel like I might be sick. The air thins and I gasp in air.

"What's wrong?" she asks.

Fuck, what was her name again?

She puts a hand on my shoulder and I jerk back. My stomach churns at the thought of rolling around with her in a bed that isn't mine. Sure, it feels good and makes me forget, but I always feel empty later.

Fuck. I feel empty already.

My high is gone and I'm crashing.

Just go in there and do her.

You'll feel better.

You'll forget what a disappointment you are to your father.

You'll forget Rose.

She wraps a hand around my bicep and squeezes. "Hey, baby, don't be shy. Let me make you feel good."

I stare down at her. Her eyes are blue when what I really want is green.

I back away from her.

"Where you going?" Her face is confused.

"I don't know, probably to hell," I mutter then take off at a run, descending the steps in the stairwell two at a time.

NINE

Rose

THE NEXT TIME I SEE Spider, it's a few days later and in the most unexpected place.

"Order's up, Rose," comes from Archie, the head order cook at Jo's Diner, a cute replica of a nineteen fifties restaurant. He slides two plates under the heat lamp, one a deluxe burger with a side of spicy fries and the other a side salad with grilled chicken.

I nod, tucking the errant strands of my French braid behind my ears. It's a weeknight and school's back in session, along with my part-time job.

Putting the plates on my tray along with drink refills, I hurry the order over to the table where Lexa and Oscar sit, pretending to do homework while they annoy me at work. I place it down in front of them.

Lexa arches a carefully drawn in dark eyebrow.

I roll my eyes. "What now?"

"H-E-L-L-O? I need ranch for my salad."

I blow at the tendrils of hair that have escaped and are tickling my forehead. "You know where it is." I point to the bar along the back wall of the diner, which is lined with soda dispensers, napkins, and a range of condiments. It's actually a pretty cool set up. "Get it yourself."

Oscar snorts. "Yeah, biotch. There are no maids here at Jo's."

I send him a grateful nod and move to the table the hostess just sat, one along the windows that line the restaurant.

I blink at the image in front of me.

Spider Wainwright sits in a booth, looking rather bemused and out of place. He's wearing jeans, a tight Vital Rejects shirt that perfectly accentuates his biceps, and a pair of black Converse.

"You," I say, pretty much at a loss for anything else.

"Me." He grins wryly and toys with the menu. Almost shyly, he looks at me, his eyes taking in my bobby socks and Keds, the rolled-up boyfriend jeans, and the black polo with Jo's red logo of a hamburger. There's a small apron tied around my waist.

The bobby socks and awful polo are a requirement to work here, and it's not exactly cute. With a permanent stench of French fries, it's the un-coolest outfit ever, but on a good night, I can make a hundred in tips alone.

"What are you doing here?" I ask.

"I came to see you."

He's here . . . in Jo's . . . and he came to see *me*.

A flurry of butterflies go crazy in my stomach.

"How did you know I worked here?"

He shrugs. "Father mentioned it when I picked up my things this week." A thoughtful look crosses his face. "He likes you. I can tell by the way he talks about you."

I stand there, trying to play it cool. "Would you like to order something?"

He looks down at the menu on the table. He's jittery, his fingers thumping against the table. "What do you recommend?"

I shove my hands in my apron pockets, fingering the cash I've collected since I started work tonight. "Our milkshakes are great."

"Mmmm, yeah," he says as he stares up at me. His eyes are on my lips.

"Would you like one?"

"What?"

I bite my lip so I won't giggle. I think I'm distracting him—and I'm not even trying. "A milkshake?"

He looks down at the menu as telltale blush works up his face. "Ah, right. Yes please, a chocolate one. And a hamburger and chips—I mean fries."

He's not as cocky as usual, and I'm baffled.

"What's up with you?" I ask.

He rubs his jaw. "Just thought I'd stop by and see a . . . friend? That is, if she still wants to be my friend?" His brown eyes are hesitant as he watches me.

"She does."

He nods. "Actually, I got some good news today, and I wanted to tell you about it."

"Oh? What is it?"

"Rose, order up," I hear Archie call from the back.

Spider looks around, as if he's rather surprised to find himself there. "It might take a while to tell you. Can you join me when my order is ready?"

I look around at my packed section. I have a four-top with two frat guys whose order is still cooking and another two-top.

I do get breaks, but never during a rush, and since it's the first week back from break, everyone is popping into Jo's to either socialize or grab dinner.

"It's too crazy in here, but I get off in two hours. We can hang out then?"

Say yes.

I want to talk to him more. I want . . .

He grimaces. "Damn. I already made plans with some friends I went to school with."

"Oh? Where are you going? Maybe I can tag along?"

At first I'm surprised by my forwardness, but then I decide it's okay. Everything with Spider seems so . . . impermanent, like he can disappear in an instant, so why not put it all out there.

He shrugs. "To a bar downtown."

"Oh."

He frowns. "It's probably not a good idea for you to join me."

"True."

Fighting my disappointment, I tell him I need to put his order in and walk away. My path takes me past Oscar and Lexa, who are furiously whispering as I approach. Lexa waves at me, her fingers pointing at Spider, her eyes big as saucers.

Oscar has the menu hiding half his face as he checks him out. Spider waves back, obviously noticing their attention.

Sweet baby Jesus. They are ridiculous.

"Is that him?" Lexa hisses once I arrive at their table.

I flare my eyes at her. "Stop ogling him."

"Oh. My. God. He is the most beautiful creature ever created. His hair . . . that tattoo . . . I want to die. Please, please, please with sugar on top will you introduce us?" Oscar says, holding his hands up in begging motion.

I gaze up at the ceiling in frustration. "You're old enough to fan-boy on your own. You don't need my help."

The bell above the door jingles as Trenton and his teammate Garrett stalk into the diner. Rich, athletic, and attractive, both are prize catches for Claremont. Aria Romero, Trenton's cousin and first-class mean girl, trails behind them. She's dating Garrett, who has the kind of face that's set in a permanent leer, and his eyes are constantly glued to my chest.

They're the upper echelon of Claremont and I'm on the bottom—not that I care.

"It's like a J.Crew ad," Oscar says with a smirk as they waltz in the door and all eyes turn toward them. "So boring. What ever happened to being an individual?"

I tap the jaunty beret he's wearing. "Not everyone's as stylish as you."

Oscar bats his lashes. "Oh, shush, you'll make me blush."

Aria's eyes sweep the room and land on us, making my hands tighten around my tray.

She's beautiful with curly brown hair, an hourglass figure, and a tongue that can flay a fish. Her eyes are ice blue and arctic.

When I first arrived at Claremont freshman year, she delighted in telling me how sorry she was that I didn't make the cut for her social club at Claremont. The Claremont Chicks didn't think my "sketchy background" would fit in with them.

Needless to say, I do my best to avoid her.

"Claremont Bitch Number One is headed our way," Oscar exclaims, saying it rather loudly as the hostess escorts them further inside. He can't stand Aria either, and I suspect it's because she targets anyone who's a little different from the norm, which certainly includes Oscar. "Let's all clap." He starts a slow, insulting clap until I brush at his hands to stop him.

Trenton's eyes find mine and he waves, his gaze sweeping over me. Blushing, I wave back. Baseball player and all-around nice guy, I've talked to him a few times since I returned, but most of it's been in class.

"Do you think Aria will be nice?" Lexa says as she straightens her shirt.

Oscar groans at her. "Why do you care so much about being in the Claremont Cunts? The school year is almost over."

He and I fist bump. "Amen," I say. "I suggest we definitely put Aria on your prayer list. She needs all the help she can get on being a decent human being."

Oscar snorts at my comment as Lexa reapplies her lipstick and talks around it. "Aria Romero is part of the group that plans Spring Fling. Maybe I want to go."

I told them about Trenton inviting me. They haven't been asked yet. Honestly, it won't be much fun if my friends aren't there.

I sigh and look at Lexa. "The best predictor of future behavior is past behavior, so it's highly doubtful she'll be nice." I pick up their now empty plates and take a step back, anxious to get away before Aria reaches the table. "I'm leaving before she gets here and we find out for sure. Bye!"

I hurry back to the kitchen to get Spider's milkshake and put in his food order while sending up a prayer that the hostess doesn't put the new trio in my section.

TEN

Rose

I COME TO A HALT as I walk out of the kitchen with Spider's shake and another order for a different table. The hostess is pulling tables together to place Lexa, Oscar, Trenton, Garrett, Aria, and Spider all together. At the same table.

I nearly drop my tray. *What did I miss?*

I make my way over to them after dropping off the other items, not missing that Aria is sitting next to Spider, closer than Saran wrap, her head bent to his as he looks at something on her phone.

Garrett glares at Spider and Aria, and I wonder if they are on or off this month. Judging by how close she is to Spider, I'm assuming they're off.

I set the shake down in front of him. "I see you found some . . . company."

Oscar grins, sitting on the other side of Spider. "I introduced myself to him"—his eyes dart to Aria—"and then the rest of them insisted on an introduction. Then, Aria suggested we all sit together."

Wasn't that nice of her?"

I look at Aria and she's smirking. "Didn't know you had a famous rock star stepbrother, Rose." She flutters her lashes. "And you probably don't know this because you're not from Highland Park, but Spider's dad and mine used to play golf together." She shoots a grin at Spider and wags her finger at him. "You had quite the reputation around here back in the day. I remember those crazy stories about you being the party guy—"

"Nice," I say, cutting her off. "It must be *super* to be from Highland Park."

Aria gives me a dark look, but I ignore her and glance at Spider, zeroing in on the part of her commentary that interested me. "Famous?"

Spider clears his throat, a gleam of excitement in his brown eyes. "It's my big news: our music video is going viral. Sebastian called today to let me know. Not only that, but radio stations are picking it up and playing our song. It's nuts." A slow grin spreads across his face. "I was going to tell you first, but apparently Aria saw it on TMZ tonight and recognized me." He grins. "It looks like "Superhero" is going to be a big hit."

Oh.

Amazement fills me, and I smile broadly—just as Aria's hand touches his shoulder.

My lips tighten.

She gestures to her phone. "Look, I found your video. It already has a million views." She holds her phone up, and I peer down at the video on YouTube where Spider and his band are playing their "Superhero" song on the rooftop of a high-rise in what looks like New York. Just like from the show, Spider is wearing his blue mink coat and those leopard print bikini underwear, showcasing his six-pack and tattoos. It's over the top, but so *him*. I watch as he struts around with his guitar, his body bending and whipping with the music. My eyes trace his sculpted chest, eagerly taking in the finely chiseled V-line where his waist disappears into his pelvis.

He's sex with a side of hard music. And it makes my heart hammer.

His arm brushes mine as he puts his hand on the table to stand so he can watch it with me. As if my body has a mind of its own, I lean closer to him. "I love that song," I murmur.

"Do you like it better than "Albatross"?" His voice is warm and right next to me, the heat from his body intoxicating. I know if I turn to face him, our faces would be inches apart.

I lick my lips. "I love "Albatross" because you sing it . . . and it's a ballad."

"I'll think about you the next time I sing it," he says softly.

"Yeah?"

"Most definitely."

It feels as if there's a current running from me to him, and if I get any closer, if I touch him, I'm going to get fried, but my body doesn't care. I turn to face him, and it's apparent we're invading the other's personal space, but neither of us seems to care. His eyes peer down at me, his gaze searching mine. My breath stalls. He's so close to me and for a moment it almost seems as if we're alone . . .

"Excuse me," Aria says, cutting into my thoughts. "Can you get us some menus, please?"

Spider seems to come out of a fog, taking a step away from me and sitting next to Aria.

I'm still recovering from the intensity of him when Trenton taps his Ray-Bans on the table to get my attention.

I almost forgot he was here.

"Hey, Rose. How's it going?" He gives me his famous hot guy chin nod. "You look great. We missed you at Jo's while you were gone."

I smile. He mentioned he'd stayed in town for the break. "That's sweet. Thank you."

Aria rolls her eyes, but Trenton doesn't see it. She's good about hiding what a real mean girl she is.

I focus back on Trenton. Tonight he's wearing a Claremont shirt, jeans, and a ball cap. Classically handsome and from a wealthy family, he could date anyone he wanted. I'm not sure why he's interested in me except that I don't chase after him or text him or try to get his attention. We had a Biology Lab together freshman year, and although he was dating someone at the time, there was a spark of attraction there. He's since broken up with that girl, and we seem to be tip-toeing around each other, deciding if we really like each other or not.

"I got my acceptance letter from NYU. I'm pretty stoked," Trenton says to me. "Did you hear back?"

I nod. "I was accepted." But that doesn't mean I'm going. I don't say that part because I don't want to be lame and I don't want to put a damper on his excitement over his own acceptance.

He stands up, obviously excited as he comes around to where I am and picks me up and gives me a hug. "That's awesome, Rose! I'm glad we'll both be there."

He eases me down and I feel the heat of Spider's gaze on me. When I look at Spider his face is inscrutable except for a telltale tic in his jaw, and I wonder what *that* means.

I think I know. He doesn't like Trenton.

Aria's voice, annoyingly shrill, cuts in. "I'm not sure what it takes to order some food around here, but I'd sure like to."

Trenton waves her off. "Hold your horses. This is great news. New York's a big city and it'll be nice to know some people there." He grins at me, his teeth straight and white against his tan skin. "Maybe we'll have some classes together."

If I get to go . . .

"How nice," Spider says, and I hear the sarcasm in his voice. Thankfully, no one else seems to notice or if they do, they don't acknowledge it.

I dart a look at him, taking in the way he's sizing up Trenton.

Trenton doesn't seem to notice because his sky blue gaze is on me.

I feel uncomfortable and I'm just about to dash off to grab some menus to get away when Oscar covers his heart with his hand. "Spider's song and Trenton's acceptance to NYU *is* incredible, but you know what would make this moment truly wonderful?"

"What?" Aria snaps as she glares at Trenton and me. She's obviously annoyed because Trenton likes me. She doesn't think I'm good enough for him. I'm tempted to stick my tongue out at her—but that's too childish. But, man, sometimes, I really want to.

"Yeah, what?" Lexa asks. She's been watching the entire interaction quietly, playing it cool.

Oscar clears his throat. "Well, seeing as Trenton invited Rose to the Spring Fling, I think it would be super special if Lexa and I were also invited?" He bats his eyes at Trenton.

I suppress a giggle. Oscar has no shame.

Trenton nods like a king. "Done. You're both invited."

Well, that was easy enough.

Aria puffs up. "We can't just go around inviting everyone, Trenton. It's an exclusive party—that's the whole point."

Trenton shrugs. "I'm the Class President, and I say they can come."

Garrett, who's been silent up to this point—I suspect because he's slow and unable to follow our conversation—decides to speak up, "Looking hot in that polo, Rosie. If I tip you big enough, do I get a private lap dance later?" He waggles his eyebrows.

Spider immediately scowls, his face hard. "Shut up, arsehole. Show some respect."

Garrett sneers. "Whatever, dude. It's Tin Town Rosie—she knows I'm just kidding, right?"

My fist tightens within the pocket of my apron at the stupid nickname. Some of the students called me that when I first arrived and it still comes back to haunt me.

"Of course. You're hilarious," I say. "But I don't give lap dances to baseball players who lost their starter status. Only the best for me."

It's no secret that the coach recently benched him. Rumor is he's been partying too much and not showing up to some of their practices.

"Crash and burn," Oscar says, tittering like an old lady as he makes an exploding sound.

Spider's face is red and tight, and I watch as he leans over the table and whispers something under his breath to Garrett. I try to hear what it is, but I can't, not with Aria in my ear. "Menus? Today?" she calls out loudly.

"Right." I flounce off and am halfway back to the kitchen when Trenton catches me at the counter. "Hey, sorry about Garrett. His mouth is out of control sometimes."

I nod.

"Why don't we go to dinner this week?" he says. "Like a real date before Spring Fling gets here."

I'm barely listening though, my eyes on Spider as Aria flirts with him.

Garrett seems to have left because I don't see him anywhere. I wonder what Spider said to him.

Just then Aria touches Spider's neck tattoo, and anger flies over me.

Ugh. I'm so jealous.

"Rose?"

I look back at Trenton, coming to a quick decision. "I'd like that."

"Good. I'm looking forward to it." He hesitates and then briefly kisses my cheek. "I'll grab the menus for our table. You do whatever you need to."

"Okay," I say, feeling rather bemused as he walks away.

I pass the rest of the night in a hurried kind of crazy, trying to get to all of my tables before my shift ends, my feet aching. My classmates order their meals then I barely check on them, instead sending my co-worker Cyndi, promising her the entire tip.

I keep a wary eye on the table as I take orders and bus tables, looking up every now and then. Each time I do, Spider meets my gaze . . . and so does Trenton.

Later, I head to the restroom to avoid saying goodbye. I barely have my hands washed when Spider walks in and closes the door behind him.

My eyes flare. "What are you doing?"

He crosses his arms, a sure sign that he is either closing himself off or feeling vulnerable. "Your friends are all arseholes—except for Oscar."

"Okay." I cross my own arms. "You seem to be having a good time with Aria."

He lets out a frustrated growl. "For someone so smart, it's interesting that you're missing what's right in front of you."

I shake my head. "What are you talking about?"

He grinds his teeth together and glares at me. "I'm at a diner . . . in a restroom that reeks of Clorox . . . to talk to a girl that . . . that . . . I like."

I grow warm. "Is that a bad thing?"

"It is when you're my stepsister and I've been warned to stay away from you." He gets a frustrated look on his face.

No. I don't want that.

"Is that what you want?"

He stares at the floor. "The only reason I came here was to see you and tell you my good news, and now I've figured out that Trenton is the guy you were reading the book for. Am I right?" He looks back up, and there's wariness in his gaze, almost as if he's preparing himself.

"Yes."

He exhales and rakes his hands through his hair. "Fuck me."

"Why do you care?"

"Nothing. Just . . . nothing."

"You're jealous," I say softly, the realization so clear that I'm giddy.

He ignores that. "And you're going to NYU with him?"

I pause, my chest tightening as I think back to my dream. "Anne won't let me. I didn't want to ruin his news, so I didn't say anything."

"But you want to go?" He studies me.

"Not for him. I want to go for me. My Granny always promised me that she and I would leave Tin Town and run away to New York." I grimace, thinking of her dying when I was ten, a year before Mama. "It was just something she said, and I guess I'm still trying to get there."

He spears me with devastatingly beautiful eyes as he palms his spider tattoo.

"What?" I ask.

He lets out a heavy sigh and rakes a hand through his hair. "I just can't stand the thought of you with him. Hate it so much it makes me want to pound on him—and don't even get me started on Garrett. I told him to leave the diner or else."

My mind is reeling from hearing this. I want to throw my arms around Spider and hug him. Maybe more.

He pivots around to head back out the door.

"Spider! Wait," I call out. "You can't leave after that."

But he doesn't turn around or stop.

Since it's the end of my shift and I don't have any more tables left, I hurriedly undo my braid and apply a quick swipe of lip gloss I have in my apron. Spider and I are going to talk.

I fly out the door just a couple minutes after him, but he's gone already.

In fact, the entire place has nearly emptied except for Oscar and Lexa. They both give me quick hugs and leave too, saying they have homework waiting on them. Cyndi comes up to me, glowing because Spider left her a hundred-dollar bill as a tip. She offers to give me half, but I sigh and say no.

I just want him, not his money.

ELEVEN

Spider

I RUN MY HAND ACROSS the dashboard of my Jeep. It might be close to six years old, but Father kept it in pristine shape while he stored it in one of his garages at the house. It brings back good memories . . . and bad. Aria was right—I was a hell raiser in prep school. I even ran away a couple of times, anything to get my father's attention.

I watch Rose as she carries her tray back to the kitchen. It appears to be the end of her shift as she busies herself cleaning up the tables.

Why does she work when she doesn't have to? I think it's admirable.

I rub at the leather wrapped around my steering wheel. She isn't like any girl I've ever met before. She has this way of looking at me like she can see every detail of my insides, as if she knows exactly what I'm thinking.

My phone rings—Sebastian. He's called me three times already today from his apartment in New York, once to tell me the news, and then two more times to update me as the views on the video kept rising.

"Dude!" he yells into my ear as I answer it. "Are you watching the views?"

"Yeah, it's sweet."

He laughs. "It's insane. And . . . get this . . . one of the music producers we were interested in called me today. He saw the video and wants to meet with us in LA."

That's huge. It's the cherry on top of the video.

"I'm ready to get to LA and just get going, you know? Find an apartment and a studio. We need so much shit!"

I grin at his exuberance.

He continues, giving me updates about the other band members. "Rocco and I are flying out to LA this weekend to look for a place to live. When's the soonest you can get there? We need to start working on the new songs for the album."

I just got here; I'm not ready to leave.

Which is funny, because normally I can't wait to get out of Dallas.

"I made this deal with my father that I'd stick around for a while. He's going to give us some startup money. You think you can wait?"

He sighs. "I don't know, man. We need to jump on this while it's hot. With this video thing going viral, Mila's already working on setting up some interviews with some shows, maybe even Kimmel. It would be nice if you were there already if we get the call."

I rub my forehead. Mila is our PR girl who mostly works for peanuts and the chance to hang out with us. We attended prep school together and since she's a trust fund girl, she has the time and money to do our promo. We're her pet project, and admittedly, she's done a fantastic job. She set up our merchandise on the website, organized the music video, and even scheduled tour stops. She's irreplaceable, and free—can't forget that. She currently lives in Dallas but wants to move to LA to be near us. I should probably go see her or call her, but I haven't yet. She has a crush on me and I don't want to encourage it.

I sigh. "My father got married, mate, and there's this girl . . ." My fingers toy with the steering wheel again. "She's different."

Different is an understatement, and I'm intensely *aware* of her, from every shift of her shoulders to the pulse in her neck.

I thought she was simply pretty.

She is fucking *luminous*.

And the best thing I can do is avoid her.

"Dude, there are beautiful girls for days in LA." His voice is light but I sense the unease. I've let him down before when I'm using . . . getting in fights or showing up to practice trashed.

I'm distracted as I watch Rose pick up her jacket from the coat rack and slip it on.

"Spider? You there?" Sebastian asks.

"Yeah, yeah. I'll work on it and let you know."

Tension crackles through the phone as his voice deepens. "I need you, man. We've spent five years on the road and it's starting to pay off. Don't let us down."

Rose exits the diner, gets in her car and pulls out of the parking lot.

"Got to go, bro. I'll call you later."

"Wait—" I hear him say, but I already ended the call.

I crank up and follow her taillights.

TWELVE

Rose

AFTER PARKING, I REACH THE sidewalk that leads up to the entrance of my dorm, cursing under my breath that the streetlight on this side of my building is out. Considering how much the tuition is—thirty thousand a year, including boarding— you'd think maintenance would do a better job. On top of that, clouds obscure the quarter moon, leaving me with almost no light. I should have brought a flashlight.

I cross the darkness quickly, eager to get to my room and hop in the shower. I get within five feet of the door close to the parking lot before I realize it's past ten, which means the side entrance will be locked and I'll have to skirt around and go in through the main lobby. *Ugh.*

I flip back around, taking the long sidewalk that winds through pretty landscaping and trees. Anxious to get to a well-lit area, I fiddle with my backpack and dig around for my keys.

A rustling sound comes from behind me.

Without pausing, my eyes scour the parking lot to my left and the darkened landscaping to my right. Nothing moves, but my pulse kicks up a beat.

You're fine, I tell myself. Besides being one of the richest neighborhoods in the world, Highland Park is also one of the safest.

With a bit more pep in my step, I focus on getting to the front door.

Another sound reaches my ears, this time a scuffling sound that stops when I do. I look over my shoulder, tingles making my scalp prickle.

Someone is out there.

Watching me.

Following me.

"Who's there?" I call, peering into the blackness.

Silence.

"I have Mace," I say. "And I'm not afraid to use it."

My hands grow clammy. I'm only about fifty yards from the main entrance. I could drop my backpack and make a dash—

"Don't freak out. It's just me, babe." I hear a chuckle and then Garrett emerges from behind a small shrub. Wearing a black beanie, he sticks his hands in his pockets and strikes a nonchalant pose, yet his steps are steady and purposeful. "I thought this was where you lived. My dorm's right next to yours. I actually saw you parking in the lot and thought I'd say hello."

Hello? Yeah, okay.

I take a step backward, my brow wrinkling. "It's late. What do you want?"

He shrugs, easing in closer and stopping about five steps from me. Over six feet tall with bulky muscles, he's intimidating.

"Nothing much. Just want to talk."

My stomach goes cold.

There's a sly tone to his voice.

I shouldn't have smarted off to him. I should have just let him get in his little snide remark about the lap dance and let it go, *pride goeth before a fall* and all that jazz.

He's reached me by now and his sharp face looms down, a sullen look flitting across his face as he rakes his eyes over me.

"I don't have time to play games, Garrett. Go find Aria if that's what you're looking for." I pivot and make to head inside, but he grabs my arm.

"Not so fast. I'm not done here."

His breath smells like whiskey, and I turn my face away and jerk my arm out of his grasp. "Don't put your hands on me—"

He holds his hands up and waves at me. "Or what, you'll tell on me? For what? I'm not doing anything wrong. We're just having a conversation."

I square my shoulders. "You're wearing a black beanie when it's seventy degrees. You followed me from the parking lot and hid in the bushes. That's what I call stalking." I say the words with bravado, but inside I'm scared. I don't really know him, don't really know what he's capable of.

All I want to do is run.

But something tells me that's what he wants.

My hands shake as I slowly inch backward toward the door. On my insistence to Anne, I've had a year of self-defense training in Krav Maga, but in this moment, I can't recall one defensive maneuver.

I swallow, running through the basics.

Don't show fear.

Keep it simple.

Be the bear.

Go for soft tissue.

My eyes dart behind me to the front door. There's a buzzer there to hit in case of trouble. If I could just reach it before he—

He jumps at me, clamps a hand around my wrists, and jerks me toward him until my chest is pressed against his. My purse falls to the sidewalk, the contents flying, including my Mace. The scent of his sweat wafts into my face. I wiggle to get away but he tugs on my scalp until my head is bent back, forcing me to look up at him. The odd angle stretches out my vocal chords, preventing me from doing anything more than wheeze as I try to scream.

My feet kick at him, searching for purchase in his groin area even as my heart races and my eyes career around, looking for help. My breathing quickens, becoming shallow and rapid.

Shit.

At this rate, I'm going to pass out.

He clenches his teeth together. "Don't ever toss baseball in my face again. You don't know shit about what you mouthed off about—"

One of my wrists wrangles free from his grip and I throat-punch him.

He staggers back and goes straight to his knees, holding his neck.

Anger and fear mingle together, making my fists curl. My chest expands as I suck in air.

Beady eyes narrow as he wheezes, getting to his feet. Before I can get my breath to run, he's already coming at me.

I widen my stance, preparing for him to tackle me—but Garrett lurches to the side as a shadow collides with him, sending him flying to the ground.

Spider is a blur as he takes him down.

Where did he come from?

His fist slams into Garrett's face, whipping it to the side. Twisting around, Garrett manages to get to his feet. Spider punches him again, this time in the stomach, causing an *oomph* to erupt from Garrett.

"Don't you ever come near her again!" Spider yells, hitting Garrett in the jaw.

Garrett curses and shakes it off, a wild look in his eyes as he rushes at Spider, knocking him down and pinning him to the ground. He gets in two good shots before Spider wriggles out from under him.

Spider lunges and jerks the beanie off, using it to wrap around Garrett's neck, whose eyes bulge. It's obvious he can breathe, but barely.

"If I ever see you within a hundred yards of her again, I'll kill you, motherfucker. You understand?" Spider bites out as he releases him, pushing him away from us with a kick to his backside. "Now get out of here, you fucking bloody arsehole, before I change my mind and beat you senseless!"

Garrett takes off across the grass, his long legs flying as he heads for the quad and the athletic dorm.

My chest heaves as Spider turns to face me. I run up to him to check him out, using my phone to get him in more light. There's a cut under his right eye and blood on his cheek.

"We need to get that looked at," I say, my heart still flying from the adrenaline.

"I'm bloody well fine." His gaze brushes over me to check me out and I can tell he's still hyped up, his eyes bouncing from my face to my arms. His chest heaves. "Did he leave bruises? Are you okay?"

I don't even know if he did. I don't care. All that matters is that I'm okay and Spider is too. I nod. "Thank you for that." I push out a laugh, adrenaline still pumping as I say, "I was doing pretty good on my own, right?" I swallow. "It felt good to throat-punch him."

"I wanted to kill him," he mumbles as he clenches his fists.

He paces around me, looking distracted and anxious. "We should call campus security."

I shake my head. "Won't work. He'll deny it and put it all on me. His family has too much money and too much influence around here. He's a superstar athlete and people will blame me somehow. Trust me, I've seen it happen time and time again. Plus, he's seventeen, and you're not."

"Fuck." He scrubs his face, his eyes uncertain. "Are you sure?"

I nod. I don't want to put him in a weird situation where he looks like the aggressor when he clearly wasn't, and part of me doesn't want this incident getting back to Robert and Anne. I know they'll judge him for it, and my protective instincts are at their highest when it comes to Spider.

I don't even know why.

I exhale, rubbing my arms. "The truth is, it's not the first time I've had to defend myself. I lived in foster care for two years before Anne came along."

"What if he tries again and I'm not here?"

"Forget him. I think you scared the shit out of him." I grab his hand, noticing that it's swelling. "Does it hurt?"

"No." He stares down at his hand as I cradle it in mine. His eyes come up to capture mine. He swallows.

I study him, recalling his earlier comment about not being able to meet me after work. "What happened to going to a club tonight?"

He takes his hand back, almost reluctantly, and lets out a breath, wiping at the blood on his face with the hem of his shirt. I get the perfect view of his hard abs and the deep V that leads down to his jeans. He's rock solid, lean, and perfect. "My plans changed . . . obviously. I followed you home from work. I would have been here sooner, but Father called me just as I parked."

Oh.

"Why did you follow me?"

He gets this cautionary look on his face. "I can't help myself when it comes to you."

Oh.

I push out a smile, still feeling off from Garrett. "Come to my room so we can get you cleaned up."

He chews on his bottom lip, the indentation of his teeth mesmerizing. "I should go."

"Maybe that would be the smart choice."

"Definitely," he says, his eyes on mine.

"But you'll come anyway," I say. "You want to."

A few seconds pass as he stares down at me, his eyes at half-mast, those lashes so thick it should be illegal. "Is my stepsister inviting me up with an ulterior motive?"

Hell yes.

Spider is a bright, hot sun and I'm Icarus, flying way too close.

"What if I said yes?"

A small smile plays around his lips. "Then I'd say show me the way."

HOW CAN ONE HUMAN MAN be so hot?

Spider sits on my toilet, shirtless, while I dab at his swollen eye. I'm doing my best to keep my eyes averted from the ink on his body, the way his tattoos swirl underneath his jeans, the way his chest is carved from stone.

Of course, I'm the stupid person who suggested he remove his shirt so I could see if he has any bruising on his chest. A cracked or broken rib can cause a lot of pain, and I want to be thorough, that's all—I swear to baby Jesus.

He grinned at my request and whipped it off—which is the reason I'm now a mess.

There's hardly any room to breathe with him in my small bathroom.

I wipe at the spot of blood on his cheek as he watches me stoically, never taking his eyes off me, tracking my every movement.

"This will look worse tomorrow," I murmur, just to ease the tension. I stand between his spread legs, acutely aware of his fresh scent, his pure magnetism. My hands shake and I have to focus to push an image of me straddling him, both of us naked, out of my head. I want to run my tongue over the tattoo on his neck. I want to bite him like an animal while he slides into me—

Good grief, Rose, stop the fantasy!

Right. I'm a virgin, and I don't have much of an idea of what happens after that anyway. Sure, I've had a couple of boyfriends, but nothing serious. I don't have much in common with the boys in Highland Park.

"You'd make a good nurse," he says softly, his long black lashes fluttering softly against his chiseled cheekbones.

"Doctor of Psychology," I correct him.

"From NYU?" His voice is inquisitive, and I guess he's over the jealous thing with Trenton and I at NYU together.

"Oscar and I both want to go. It's . . . everything to me."

"Your dream?"

"Yes." Although right now I'm dreaming of him . . .

"I know that feeling. That's how music is to me." His golden-brown eyes watch me as I reach over to the medicine cabinet for more antiseptic and antibacterial cream, my chest perilously close to his face. I swear my nipples are reaching for him.

"Why psychology?"

I nod, pretending like I'm not all discombobulated. "My granny mainly. She loved to read people—literally. She ran a little palm-reading business out of her home before she died. All the old ladies of the neighborhood would come to talk to her. She'd make them coffee and they'd just . . . talk, and then she'd tell them what they needed to hear while I sat on the floor next to her and listened. There wasn't any magic involved of course." I laugh. "But . . . she was incredibly intuitive. She just got people. If someone twitched or looked left or right while they were talking, she'd have a reason for it and she'd tell me all about it after they left."

He smiles. "How on earth did you get to Highland Park?"

"Through foster care, until Anne." I toss the cotton ball I used to dab at his eye into the trash.

"What happened to your real parents?" There's softness in his gaze, as if he's felt the pain of being alone.

I sigh. "Well, Granny raised me, but she died when I was ten. The lady who gave birth to me had gotten pregnant by a man who ran off a few months later, so I've never met my real dad. The last I heard, he was in prison in Florida. The only guy I knew was Mama's boyfriend Lyle. One night he hit her a little too hard and broke her neck." I inhale sharply at the memory. "The cops pulled him over for questioning, and he pulled a gun on them. One of the cops shot him and he died too."

His face has hardened as I speak, and I clear my throat. "I'm not a victim, so don't get that in your head. Granny raised me to look for the good in everyone and to never let the past get me down. She said it didn't matter where I was from, just where I was going—and I'm going places. I'm getting out of this town if it's the last thing I do."

"I think I would have loved your granny." He curls an arm around me, tugging me close until my chest is a hair's breadth away from his face. I recall our epic kiss on the plane. I feel the pressure of his taut thighs and my breath quickens as desire unfurls inside me, wrapping me up and inching me closer to him.

"I don't doubt for an instant that you'll be a doctor someday," he murmurs. "You've got a chip on your shoulder, which means you'll fight tooth and nail. You're a tad bitter and have people to prove wrong. I see it on your face." He smiles wryly. "Obviously you're not the only one who likes to analyze people." His full, sensuous lips curve into a smile.

A hum warms my blood. I want him—desperately.

And it's entirely foolish.

He's my stepbrother.

He doesn't call girls back.

"How do you know so much about me?" I ask, feeling myself gravitating closer.

He thinks about it, pushing a piece of hair out of my eyes. Cupping my nape, he pulls me in tighter until our noses meet. The back of his hand caresses my cheek and the heat from his touch burns, yet there's a tautness in the roped muscles of his arms, as if he's holding himself in check.

"Because I am you," he says softly. "We're so much alike, it's staggering." He pauses and stares deep into my eyes. "With one exception: you're better than me. I tossed away my teenage years on drugs and booze." He bites his lip. "I'm still doing it. I can't stop, Rose. Some days I want to stop—*fuck*, I really do—but I've never had anything that was *enough* to give me the strength to do it. Does that make sense?"

I nod. I can't think. He's so close to me, his eyes burning into mine as he tries to get across what he means.

He closes his eyes and exhales. "I want you, Rose. You're intoxicating."

I suck in a sharp breath, our lips inches apart.

Is he going to kiss me? I want him to.

His eyes open after the silence has gone on too long, a smirk forming around his mouth. "You scared of me, Rose?"

Never.

"I'm scared you'll rip my heart out."

He stares at the LOST tattoo on his hand. "I probably will."

He stands, and my small bathroom shrinks even more. Inhaling a steadying breath, I stuff everything back in the cabinet and lead him into my bedroom.

He looks around the space, still bare-chested, taking in my small corner room. His gaze lingers on the full-sized bed then moves to the desk and my wall of books. Pictures of the Brooklyn Bridge and the Empire State Building are my only art.

"No roommate?" he asks as he picks up a photo of Oscar, Lexa, and me at the Friends of the Library mixer last year.

"No. It's private, one of the perks of having Anne on the school board."

He runs his fingers along my collection of paperbacks. "Which one's your favorite?"

I move to stand next to him and pull out the dog-eared copy of *Jane Eyre* by Charlotte Brontë then press it into his hand. "You should read it."

His brow arches. "Maybe I already have."

I get excited. "Really?"

He laughs. "No, sorry. Am I not as cultured as you thought now?"

"It doesn't matter. Read it now. Take it, please, as a gift from me to you."

He cocks his head as he thumbs through the pages, some of which I've highlighted and underlined. "Why? What's it about?"

"An orphan girl who searches her whole life for love. It's about how she finds it, finally, in the arms of a man she's been told she can't have."

His chest expands as he looks from me to the book. "You have a lot of attachment to this character?"

I nod. "She's poor and struggles with other people's low opinion of her social class." I pause, feeling unexpected emotion tugging at me. "I-I guess I want what Jane gets at the end of the book: happiness in spite of everything she's been through. She deserves it. I deserve it."

He studies me, awe in his gaze, the emotion so apparent that right then, I lose my heart.

"You'll find it," he says. "Someday, Rose. I promise."

I swallow. "Perhaps I already have."

His expression changes, becoming torn.

"What?" I ask.

"Nothing." He shakes his head.

I touch his arm, letting my hand drift down to his fingers. I'm tired of pretending. "Spider . . . there's something here between us. You know it."

He exhales, staring at the floor for a few ticks before raising his head to meet mine. His cheeks flush a lovely color, and I start.

Confident and cocksure Spider is shy—by his feelings for me?

The world really is tilting on its axis.

"I don't want to rehash old shit, but I want you to know that I'm really sorry for . . . what happened on the plane with the flight attendant. It's what I do—let people down constantly. Just ask anyone. You're a sweet girl, Rose . . . too sweet for me."

My heart aches. "I don't want to talk about the flight attendant. It's over."

He looks up. "I hurt you."

"We didn't even know each other," I say, trying to put the thoughts away. I want to box those images up, throw them into the ocean, and then pile a bunch of cement rocks on top. "Let's forget we met that way."

He nods, raking his hand through his hair and tugging on the ends. "Start fresh, you mean? Friends, like I said in the diner? I'd like that."

I close my eyes. *Friends* is not quite right. I want . . . hard and wild and reckless.

He doesn't wait for me to answer.

I don't know why.

Maybe it's what he sees on my face.

He exhales. "I'm only twenty-two, but I know a lot about losing people, Rose. I lost my sister to an early grave. I lost my mum when she ran away to be with someone else, and I lost my dad even longer ago. I don't let people leave me anymore, and you . . . you have just a little bit of power over me. It's enough that it messes with my head. I need calm and music and my band mates. Do you understand?" His voice is excruciatingly soft, the words chipping away at the fragile glass that is my heart.

I understand perfectly. He's letting me down easy.

I suck in a deep inhale.

"I'm sorry about Cate."

He leans his shoulder against the wall and crosses his legs, studying me.

"If you ever want to talk about her, I'm here for you."

He falters and studies his hands, a tremor there. "I let go." Pain flits across his face. "I let her go. It's my fault she's gone."

I get queasy at the images his words bring up as I start to understand. I don't know how Cate died, but my imagination is going crazy. "You let her go?"

He looks up and nods, his face a wasteland.

"What do you mean?" I ask.

He rakes his hand through his hair, his teeth chewing at his bottom lip. "We'd been warned to stay off a lake that had frozen over. I didn't listen, of course, and partially fell in. I was fine . . . I managed to get myself out of the water, but she came out to check on me, and slipped and . . ." He trails off.

"She fell in?" Horror washes over me.

He nods, his throat working as he swallows convulsively. "The ice cracked wide open when she fell, and she went completely under. I tried to pull her out . . . but she kept slipping off. She was so cold . . . and I held on to her hand as long as I could. I tried to pull her out, but I wasn't strong enough. I screamed and yelled for help, but there wasn't anyone around." His eyes close and I see wetness there. He sucks in a shuddering breath. "Our hands just . . . slipped apart."

Cold fills me up, and I feel breathless as if I am there in the moment, watching it happen with him.

Resignation settles on his slumped shoulders. "My father blames me."

"No," I whisper. "He can't. Why would he? It was an accident. You were kids."

"You're too nice, Rose."

"I'm not, you know." I pause. "I want my stepbrother."

His eyes find mine, and I'm not sure how long we stand there, staring at the other.

A bolt of electricity shoots from me to him and my lower body is hot. I want him pressed against my skin.

His gaze lingers on my lips then slides back to my face.

I want to go to him, to wrap my arms around him, but he moves first, wrapping his arms around me and clutching my head to his shoulder. "It's time for me to go."

No!

I'm a mess of emotions, scared of everything he makes me feel. Scared of how lost he is.

His chest heaves as he releases me. Warm, tattooed hands cup my cheeks. "Lock the door behind me, and if that guy even so much as looks at you, call me." He steps back to scribble his number on a slip of paper and place it on my desk.

"Don't go," I whisper as he moves to the door. "Stay."

He doesn't respond, but his face says everything. I see torment. I see indecisiveness. It's just as hard for him to walk away as it is for me to watch him go.

I can't breathe.

He's leaving me.

He opens the door, slips outside, and is gone.

THIRTEEN

Rose

THE NEXT DAY, AS RUMORS about Garrett's black eyes begin to circulate around school, I mentally prepare myself for a possible retaliation.

It happens before my calculus class after lunch. Aria stomps up to me at my locker—as well as she can in her high heels—and lets me have it, her high-pitched, shrill voice echoing down the concrete halls as she tells me what an awful person I am for letting my stepbrother beat Garrett up.

"It was clear to everyone that you were coming on to him at the diner," she says, her hands on her hips. "And thanks to you, the baseball coach has kicked him off the team for fighting."

"He was wearing a beanie and hiding in the woods." How much more does she need to know? "He's an idiot."

Her eyes are cold. "I'm going to do everything I can to make sure you and your little group of misfits are disinvited to Spring

Fling. Trenton is crazy to even want you there."

My teeth snap together. I don't care so much for me, but Oscar and Lexa will be devastated.

She tosses her hair back. "I don't know why he even likes you."

My hands curl around my books. God, I'm sick of this place. I'm sick of girls like Aria. Mostly, I just want to run away and find a place where I belong . . . somewhere, anywhere that isn't here.

Oscar's face appears next to me and his nose is scrunched up as if he smells bad fish. "Having some trouble?"

"No," I say, not taking my eyes off her. "I've got this. Aria was just leaving."

Aria rakes her eyes over the black leather duster he's sporting on top of his school khakis and white button-up shirt. She grimaces. "You are so weird," she spits disdainfully before flouncing off.

"What a little bitch," he says, following her with his eyes before turning to me. "You okay?"

I nod. I don't want to tell him about the party.

"You know I really don't care about that party, right?" he says as if he's read my mind.

I arch my brow and he chuckles. "Okay, I care, but if this episode with Garrett makes you feel uncomfortable, then we can just ditch it and do our own thing."

"And miss out on the champagne fountain and the DJ? Sad." I smirk.

"Don't forget the copious amounts of drunk people we can make fun of."

"They're all assholes."

He smirks. "Not us."

I laugh and hug him. No matter what the rest of this year

brings, I'm glad I have him.

AFTER SCHOOL, I DASH TO my dorm, where I quickly discard
my plaid skirt and white shirt, exchanging them for my jeans and
another black polo. I'm in a rush and barely have time to braid
my hair before I'm out the door and off to work, which I'm oddly
looking forward to. I need the distraction to keep me from thinking
about Spider.

I've just gotten to my car when Trenton's deep voice reaches
me. "Rose! Wait up!"

Great. I managed to not see him all day because I'm worried
about how he's going to react to the whole Garrett incident, but
now here he is. I paste on a smile then turn and watch him jog
toward me.

As he gets closer, I soften. With his wavy, sandy blond hair
and strong physique, he's easy to watch.

"I've been chasing you all day," he says as he comes to a halt
in front of me.

I can't help but smile. "Did you run clear across campus to
find me?"

He nods. "I went to your dorm, and the girl downstairs at
the desk said you'd just left." He stares down at me, a little frown
between his eyes. "Are you avoiding me?"

I shift from one foot to the other. "You know about Garrett,
right?"

He gives me a quick nod. "You okay?"

"Thanks to Spider." I twist my lips. "The gossip is Garrett got
kicked off the team. I assumed you might be upset with me about

that since you're his teammate."

Trenton gives me a serious once-over. "It's you I'm worried about. I like you, Rose, a lot."

I fiddle with my backpack.

He comes a bit closer, his scent like sea air and ocean breezes. "Garrett and Aria happened to be at my house the other night when I mentioned coming to Jo's. They tagged along, and I wish they hadn't."

He's saying the right things, and my heart likes it.

But . . . Spider.

"And . . . I've warned him personally to give you a wide berth."

I think about Oscar and Lexa. "So we're all still invited to the party?"

"Of course." He looks flummoxed that I would even suggest it. I don't bring up Aria's comments; she's his family, and I don't want to get in the middle of that.

A few hours later, I am just setting down food on a four-top when Spider walks in the door. I nearly trip over a customer's leg as I watch him take the same booth he was in last night.

He's here! my heart rejoices.

Don't get excited! my head retorts.

As soon as I get the table their drink refills, I straighten my apron and head his way. He has a small bruise under his eye but it's not nearly as bad as Garrett's.

He watches me, his gaze not moving from my face, and I find that the way he looks at me, so intently, is one of the reasons I find him incredibly intoxicating. It's as if he's studying me and taking notes.

I smile at him and he smiles back. "You're okay from last night, right? Anything happen at school today?"

I wave him off. "Things are fine. Aria was weird, but don't worry about me. How's the famous YouTube video?"

His eyes brighten. "Sebastian's been calling me every few hours with updates—like I can't see for myself that it's going crazy. The Ellen Show called, or tried to, I think. It's going to be . . . big."

"Of course it is. You're incredibly talented."

There's a long pause as we stare at each other, and I clear my throat. "So, can I get you anything?"

He lets his eyes drift over me, lingering on my lips. "Uh, yeah. Actually, I came to talk about this." He pulls out the copy of *Jane Eyre* I gave him. "I stayed up until three this morning reading this bad boy. I didn't finish, but I'm blaming you for the bloody bags under my eyes."

"And the bruise?"

He chuckles.

My excitement is so high that I have to keep myself from yelling out, *I got Spider to read Jane Eyre! Booyah!*

"What did you think?" Before I even know what's happening, I'm sitting across from him.

He considers me. "I think . . . Jane is strong. I'm half-way in love with her already."

Oh.

My stomach flutters and I swallow. "And Rochester? What do you think about him?"

"He's an arsehole who's wrapped up in his past mistakes, and that crazy wife of his is insane." He bites his lip. "I'm at the part where he wants Jane to be his mistress. It's . . . tense."

My body gets hot, imagining him as Rochester and myself as Jane. I picture us somewhere in England, curled up in front of a fire that burns in the bedroom of our large estate. I'm wearing a white gown, and he's laying me down and taking my virginity—

I come back as Spider asks, "Does she want him as much as he wants her?"

My heart skips a beat. "Yes," I say breathlessly.

"Tell me how it ends," he says. "Does he ever get over Jane? Does she go to India with that bloody awful tosser St. John? Does Rochester's wife kill them all? Fuck—will these people ever be happy?"

All of a sudden, it feels like we aren't talking about the book at all.

Impulsively, I reach out and touch his hand. It seems to be the norm for me when it comes to him. I have no self-control. "Love wins if you let it."

My eyes are telling him more.

At first, he looks confused; then he seems torn as he leans back in his seat, the action pulling his hand away from mine. He clears his throat and looks around the room. I can see he's retreating.

I don't want him to.

"I should probably head out," he says, sliding the book back inside his leather jacket. "I told Father I'd come by and talk to him about LA. He knows a lot of people there."

It sounds genuine, but it feels like an excuse.

In the background, I hear the jingle of the bell and the sound of the cook's voice as he shouts that an order is up.

I sigh and I'm about to stand up when an arm is tossed around my shoulder and Trenton slides into the booth next to me. He gives me a quick squeeze.

"Hey gorgeous."

I blink and look at him, bringing myself back to reality. "Hey!"

He throws Spider a glance and a quick greeting, but it doesn't matter because Spider is already standing and scowling down at us. His face is pale as he pivots around and marches out the door, leaving me feeling winded and very *what the hell just happened*.

"Was it something I said?" Trenton asks, his eyes studying my face.

I shake my head. "No, don't worry about it. He's just . . . in a hurry, I guess."

In a hurry to stay away from me . . .

FOURTEEN

Rose

GO THROUGH THE REST of the week weighed down by a rock in my gut.

Spider consumes all my thoughts.

I try tossing him out of my head. I go to dinner with Trenton and let him kiss me. I hang out with Oscar and Lexa at the library. I work an extra shift at the diner for Cyndi just to keep myself busy. I even attend a study group for my calculus class that's kicking my ass, but nothing works to eject him from my brain.

Anne and Robert arrange another family meal on Friday evening. I look forward to it anxiously, planning on wearing a pair of white slacks and a yellow silk tank with a cream sweater that Anne bought for me at one of her favorite stores. Oscar is in the room when I pick it out and he calls it a "rich old lady outfit", but I don't care. I'll wear anything as long as I get to see Spider.

I dress in the silk tank and the pants in the bathroom then dash out to the bedroom to let Oscar have a look. I've put my hair up in a sleek ponytail, and I do a little twirl for him.

Oscar gives his approval and I head to Highland Park for dinner.

It's not until I get there that I discover Spider isn't coming. I eat my dinner, feeling disappointed and just . . . bereft. It's that state of mind that prompts me to bring up the NYU issue again, this time with Robert present.

Anne's back goes ramrod straight. "We've had this discussion already. I don't want you so far away."

"But why?" I need a freaking good reason!

Her lips tighten. "You need supervision, Rose."

Her words sting me.

"I'm almost eighteen," I blurt. "I can go to college in another state if I want to."

She shakes her head. "I'm only paying for Winston. It only makes sense that you attend a school nearby so I can supervise you. Plus, that way you can still speak at the galas. Don't you want to help those kids?"

My jaw tightens at her manipulations. "Of course I do, but you're trying to make me feel guilty about wanting to go away to college, Anne."

"I don't like your attitude," she says sharply. "Please use a respectful tone when you talk to me."

Here we go with the manners . . .

I set down my dessert spoon and stand, needing to get out of here.

"You haven't been excused," she says, wiping her mouth.

Robert shoots her a soft look. "Rose probably has plans, dear. It's a Friday night."

She lets out a breath and nods. "Fine. It's obvious you need some time to cool down anyway."

I'm about to go but decide to turn back around, my anger too sharp to let go. "Make no mistake, Anne, I know exactly who I am—and I don't need supervision. I lived a whole life before I ever met you. I took care of myself when Mama didn't. I kept myself away from Lyle. By the time you came along, I'd seen things you can never imagine."

Her mouth compresses. "Enough of that."

I shake my head and clench my fists, trying to not raise my voice when all I want to do is yell. "And by the way, I've already applied to NYU and been accepted. Whether you pay for it or not, I'm going to New York."

She inhales a sharp breath, her hand on her stomach.

I give them a brief look and stalk out of the dining room. I'm running on adrenaline as I get in my car then squeal out of the driveway and away from Highland Park.

Before I realize where I'm going, I'm headed to Robert's penthouse in the city, where Spider is staying.

The doorman recognizes me from when I helped move some of Anne's things and greets me warmly as he escorts me to the elevator.

With nervous fingers, I push the button for the penthouse, my eyes taking in the opulence of the mirrored walls. The elevator comes to a halt, easing open to a marble-tiled floor. I hear music vibrating through the steel front door.

I knock.

And knock again.

The music is turned down and I hear rustling sounds from behind the door.

"It's me," I say. "The girl you've been avoiding."

The door swings open, and the guy standing there isn't Spider.

He's around Spider's age with scruff on his chiseled jawline and wild blond hair that flows off his face like a lion's mane. He's wearing a pair of athletic shorts and a tank top, and sweat drips from his forehead.

Ice blue eyes crinkle in the corners as they study me.

I give it right back and rack my brain, trying to recall why he seems so familiar.

I snap my fingers. "Sebastian? Lead singer of the Vital Rejects?"

"Yeah, angel." He wipes at his forehead and leans against the doorjamb, sending me a cocky grin. "And you must be *the girl*." He waggles his eyebrows.

The girl? With emphasis?

What does that even mean?

Has Spider been talking about me?

"Back away from my stepsister, douchebag," comes Spider's voice from down the hall, although I don't see him. He must be in another room.

"Fuck off," Sebastian yells over his shoulder. "You forgot to mention how hot she is."

"Watch it. I'll beat your arse if you touch her," Spider warns him in a sharp tone, and I feel a blush coloring my cheeks. I guess that answers the question of whether or not he's been talking about me.

Sebastian opens the door farther and nods his head toward the interior of the apartment. "Come on in. He'll be out in a minute. He's got to get gorgeous before we go out."

"Oh?" *They're going out?*

Probably to a bar . . . where there are older girls . . . and alcohol.

Activities I can't participate in.

Suddenly I'm rethinking everything. I shouldn't have come.

But, I've come this far, and I need to see him. I follow Sebastian into the apartment and stand uncertainly in the den as he gets me a soda from the fridge.

I pick at the sides of my jeans. "Where are you guys headed?"

Before Sebastian can reply, Spider saunters into the room, and my powers of speech leave me for a moment.

"Your hair . . . it's white," I whisper when I finally regain my faculties, my eyes greedily moving over his sweptback style. The bleached strands perfectly frame his face, accentuating the sharpness of his cheekbones, the darkness of his eyes, the long tan column of his throat. My chest squeezes at the sight of him. How can one guy be so dang hot? It's not fair to the rest of the fucking world. "What happened to the blue?"

He touches it. "It's a throwback, but always a favorite. You like it?"

"Yes," I say, my voice breathless.

I take a step back, my legs bumping into the couch, causing me to suddenly sit. I don't mind because I feel like something big is happening, and I just needed to grasp hold of it and own it.

"You okay?" he asks. "You look weird."

I shake my head, thinking . . . about a boy with white hair.

The accent.

That devil-may-care shrug.

A distant memory reaches out and tugs me into the past. There I am, at the back of the Quickie Mart. I swallow, my head burdened by things I locked in a coffin with Mama years ago.

I see my mother on the floor, dark bruises on her neck.

I see . . . a beautiful boy.

HIM.

Sebastian and Spider are both eyeing me and then each other, but I ignore them as I pull my cell phone out of my purse and dial a number, one emblazoned on my brain and on my body.

I push in the digits, but like it always did before, the call goes to a disconnected line.

Even so, it must be him.

It must be.

Years may have blurred his face in my childlike memory, but it's all coming back now. "What's going on?" Sebastian looks confused. "Are you trying to call someone?"

I come to a decision and focus on Sebastian. "I don't know you, and I hate to be rude, but can you please leave us alone for a bit?"

Spider sends him a quick nod and Sebastian straightens his tall form, his gaze reading me. Whatever he sees makes him act. "Gotcha. I'm outie. Call me later Spider." He walks out of the apartment, the door shutting softly behind him.

"Is everything okay?" Spider asks me.

I shake my head as I shrug out of my sweater. I pull my silk tank up and over my head, tossing it on the hardwood floor. He inhales sharply, his gaze going straight to my white lace bra.

"Rose, put your shirt back on." His voice is steady, but his eyes—*oh God*—those eyes are burning.

"No." I march over toward him and he backs up against the wall.

"Rose?" His chest expands, and I know he's breathing me in.

"I know you." My voice is soft, aching with memories, wanting him to see. "From Tin Town . . . when I was eleven and you were sixteen. You were at the Quickie Mart and you gave me three hundred dollars. It was the morning after Mama died. You . . . you gave me your cell phone number and told me to call you if I ever needed you."

There's a dawning in his eyes.

Lifting my hair up with my hands, I turn around to show him my back. I know what he sees: the butterfly tattoo on my upper back, inked in orange, green, and purple. Although small, his cell number is etched inside the swirls of the right wing.

"The butterfly . . . it's in memory of you, a reminder of the boy who flitted by for an instant and gave me hope and then was gone, flying away somewhere else. I-I got it done in New York. Your old cell is inside the wings."

I can't see his face, but I hear him inhale as he traces the numbers with light fingers. My body shivers as goose bumps rise at his touch.

There is a deep silence as he processes this.

I don't mind it.

His voice is filled with awe. "That's my old number. My father disconnected it when I didn't go to college. How do you—" His voice stops. "I remember you. You were hungry."

I turn back around and face him, gazing up into those fathomless eyes, the ones I carried in my heart for years. I repeated those digits over and over in my head when I was faced with mean foster siblings, hungry nights, or just plain loneliness.

His eyes meet mine and we stare at each other.

My brain knows he's going to be a rock star. It's plain as the nose on my face that he's going to break my heart.

But I can't let him go.

I take a deep inhale, my eyes still clinging to his. "Staring at someone for longer than six seconds signals that you either want to have sex with them or murder them. Which one is it?"

He closes his eyes, and I weave my hands into his white hair, tugging on the ends as our lips come together.

He hesitates slightly and then groans, his hands going to my ass and pulling me against him.

With a swift movement, he flips me around until I'm the one against the wall and he's in control. He kisses me back hard with a desperation that says he's afraid I might disappear in the space of a heartbeat. There's scruff on his jaw and it rubs my face and throat as his lips work me over, devouring me.

He wrenches himself from me, his breathing ragged, his shoulders quivering as if he's holding himself back with the utmost restraint.

"Don't stop," I say.

My body gravitates toward his, my breathing shallow as a swell of emotions flies at me. I go in to take his lips again but he holds me at bay, leaning his forehead against the wall behind us.

He finally speaks, his voice rough as if it's been dragged over rocks. "I told Father I'd leave you alone, but I can't."

"Thank God."

He raises his head and looks at me, and I feel like I've ensnared him, captured him. I feel like a siren that calls sailors to jump from their ships and worship them forever.

"You're too good for me," he says, his hand lightly touching my shoulder before dipping down to caress my arm. His lips hover over mine . . . waiting.

"I'm not. I want you just the way you are. I don't care about anything else." I trace the outline of his lips, pulling on the bottom one until he groans. I take his mouth, my tongue nipping at his, inhaling his scent of spice and leather. I'm rough with him because I want it rough back. I want his desperation. I want his need.

He groans my name and pushes down the straps of my bra

until my breasts spring free. His mouth encircles one of my nipples and tugs as his hand cups the other, tweaking it with his thumb. "You're so beautiful. I want to touch you everywhere."

"Yes," I moan.

He kisses the side of my neck and sucks the skin. "I want to fuck you, Rose. I have since the moment I saw you." His voice is guttural and harsh, and his dirty word makes my core clench.

"I'm not stopping you."

My hands go to his jeans and unsnap them, reaching in to wrap my hands around his hard cock, my fingers sliding up his velvet skin.

He hisses, his mouth claiming mine once again.

Amidst our heavy breathing, his shirt disappears as he whips it over his head. I kiss my way down the hollow of his throat while he slips his hand inside my pants and underneath my underwear. I'm wet as he touches me, sliding in and out.

Everything moves in a blur as we melt into each other, grasping and kissing.

In a blink we are in a bedroom, our clothes gone, our skin touching in places that makes me moan and arch my hips toward him with need.

We lie on top of a white feather comforter and he hovers over me. I wiggle closer, needing him inside me. Part of me wants to rush, to get the painful part over.

"Are you a virgin?" he asks, his brown eyes hot yet hesitant.

I nod, and he lets out an exhale. "I want to say I'm sorry for taking it from you, but I'm glad it's me and not Tren—"

I put a finger to his lips. "It's you. Always you."

He runs a long finger down my cheek, his brown eyes holding mine, an anxiousness there that makes my heart flutter even more.

"Before we do this . . . will you come to LA with me?" he whispers. "I want you with me, Rose. All the time."

What about New York? I think for half a second, but then he kisses me.

I want to be with him. He's my butterfly.

"I'll follow you anywhere," I say.

He kisses me again, his lips hot, his hands hotter as he touches my center, preparing me for him. I writhe and beg him to hurry.

Neither of us hears our parents walk into the room.

FIFTEEN

Spider

"**Y**OU SAID YOU'D LEAVE HER alone," my father yells as we face off against each other in the kitchen of the flat. He glares at me as he paces around the penthouse. I sit on a barstool with no shirt on, drinking the watery Jack and Coke Sebastian left out for me before everything went to hell.

I set the glass down and rake a shaking hand through my hair, tugging on the ends. *Fuck.* I really screwed things up now.

Rose has already left, whisked away by Anne as soon as she threw her clothes on.

God, her face.

It was white as a sheet.

She was mortified . . . and calling my name.

What a cluster fuck.

"You're a bloody liar who can't keep his hands to himself," Father tosses out as I take another drink and slam my glass on the counter.

"You can leave any time," I grind out.

"This is *my* penthouse." His lips tighten. "Whether it's women or drugs or booze, you always take too much." He shakes his head. "By the way, the housekeeper found the coke you left in the bathroom upstairs. You go too far, Clarence. Too far."

"Piss off." I scrub my face.

Rose.

That's all I can see.

Her face. Those eyes that look at me like I am a fucking hero.

Far from it—I am a goddamn mess.

I'm not fit for anyone—not like this, not really.

I clench my fists. *What have I gotten her into?*

I need a bump.

I need a hit.

I need anything.

I need Rose.

My heart cracks, fucking breaks in my chest, and I want to rip open my body and yank it out. Instead, I jerk up and pace around the room, opting to make myself another drink and suck it down. Father watches me warily, his lips flat.

Sebastian walks in the door and comes to an abrupt halt, a look of confusion on his face as he takes in the scene. His gaze sweeps the place, looking for Rose. He showed up here yesterday to check on me and convince me to pack my bags and come to LA with him now instead of later.

Father turns his gaze to him, his voice lower than when he spoke to me. "This is a private conversation, Sebastian."

Sebastian takes one look at my face and stands his ground. "I understand, but I think I'll stay, sir. Spider may need me."

I exhale. Sebastian is the best mate I have. He's always been right here with me since prep school days, picking up the pieces. I don't deserve him either. I don't deserve shit.

"He walked in on us."

Sebastian's face pales. "Shit." Ignoring my father, he comes over and puts a hand on my shoulder. "You good?"

I nod my head.

Then I shake it. "No." My stomach hurts, and the look on Rose's face when she walked out wrecked me. I clench my fists together and rub my eyes. "I fucked up. I need to go find Rose."

A long breath comes from Sebastian. "Spider . . . dude . . . think long and hard about that. She's a kid, and you're on your way out of town. Maybe . . . maybe this is how it's supposed to be."

My father chimes in. "Do you have any idea what this could do to Anne . . . to our relationship?"

I look at him and there's worry mingled with anger etched on his face.

"I'm just bad luck for you, aren't I?" I say.

Cate, my eyes say. *Mum.*

He exhales and holds his hands up. "It's not like that, Spider. This is just a fresh start for me. For us—if you want it to be."

I shrug and look away from him. I don't want to think about fresh starts.

He tugs on his tie, loosening it. "I wasn't around when you were young, but this thing with Anne . . . I love her . . ." He trails off.

What about me?

Ignoring him, I stalk past him and outside to the balcony where I pull a cigarette from my pocket and light it up, sucking in the nicotine.

I hear Father and Sebastian talking quietly inside, but I tune them out.

I've smoked five cigarettes when I feel my father join me even though I don't look at him. He's made his own drink and is sipping on a Scotch, a visible tremor in his hand. He lets out a deep exhale. "I can tell you think highly of Rose, and maybe this is more than just one of your usual—"

I send him a withering look. "Don't. You don't know anything about me," I bite out.

He nods, that cool English exterior of his in full force. "Indeed. You're right, I don't know you, because we never spent much time together. I barely had time for you when you were a baby. Your sister died, your mum left, and I carried on like nothing had changed. I dumped you at a boarding school in a foreign country and went to work. It was terribly wrong of me, and my only excuse is . . . well, I didn't know how to be what you needed. I'm sorry for it. I feel partly responsible for the situation you currently find yourself in—using drugs and thinking you're in love with an underage girl."

I clench the railing of the balcony. I can't believe he just said all that. I spear him with a look, glad he said it. It makes it real. "I think that just about covers it." I pause. "After Mum left, I saw you six times in four years. That's fucked up."

He nods. "I can do better. I want to."

We stand there in the wind, watching the cars move below. I think about the past, about how unhappy my father has probably been since Cate and Mum.

I exhale a deep breath. "Believe it or not, I'm . . . glad for you." I wave my hands at him. "Anne and the baby. You deserve a second chance."

A strained, pensive look flits across his face as he sticks his hands in his pockets and stares out at the skyline. "Every day is a second chance, son. All you have to do is take it."

I slide my eyes to his, gauging his reaction. "Maybe Rose is what I need."

A firmness settles on his face. "There's only one thing that's certain in this situation, and it's that you need to get out of her life."

I know he's right.

There's a side of me that also feels disappointed in myself, in my inability to leave her alone. I rub my forehead.

"Can I bum a cig?" he asks.

He hasn't smoked since I was in diapers, at least not that I've seen. I pass one to him and he lights it like a pro, cupping the flame against the wind.

"I don't think I really know you at all," I say, watching him.

He nods as his eyes study me. "Same."

I'm suddenly overwhelmingly tired. "What do you want from me?"

He takes a long drag, his brows knitting together as if he's thinking hard. "I have a proposition for you," he says, leaning over the balcony and staring off into the horizon. "I've been talking to Sebastian about something, and I think I have a plan, one that will work out well for everyone involved."

I pause. "Including Rose?"

He nods. "Especially Rose."

I nod. He tells me his idea, and before he's even finished, I know it's the right thing to do.

SIXTEEN

Rose

"**Y**OUR BEHAVIOR IS COMPLETELY UNACCEPTABLE," Anne says from the counter in the kitchen as she pours herself a glass of iced tea. "I won't let you throw yourself away on some thug." Even though she's clearly rattled, her words are spoken without drama. That's just her.

Don't respond, I tell myself. *You'll only make it worse. She's a judgmental person; you can't change her mind.*

I sit at the breakfast table, my hands clenched under the table, holding myself together. We've been sitting here for half an hour and my head throbs. Apparently, Anne used an app on my phone to track where I went after I left her house and saw that I was at the penthouse. She and Robert came over to see why.

"You were in bed with him." She inhales a sharp breath.

Shame colors my face and I stare down at the table. "We didn't have sex."

I flick my eyes over to check my phone to see if he's texted me.

"Put your phone away, Rose."

I turn it facedown. "Sorry."

She sits down across from me, her face pale. "You will not see him again." Her words are little bells that can't be un-rung . . . clear, cold, and final.

"That's going to be hard since you're married to his dad. I will see him," I say, gripping the edge of my seat.

She shakes her head. "I didn't want to tell you this, but the housekeeper found drugs in his room from the night he was here."

I'm surprised but not shocked. "I don't care," I say. He and I will figure it out.

Her lips part. "You don't know what you're saying. If you get caught up with him . . . well, you'll get messed up too . . . like your mother."

I am *nothing* like my mother.

I'm almost damn perfect considering where I came from.

"I'm not like her. I'm like Granny."

"You can't act like anyone from Tin Town, even your Granny," she says sharply.

I can't let her put Granny in her category of people from Tin Town.

I stand, the storm that's been whipping in me sweeping to the surface. "It doesn't matter where I'm from. All that matters is where I'm going."

I snatch my phone off the table and text him. My heart is racing. I need to get out of here.

Please come get me. I need you. I'm at the house.

Anne sighs and stands to take her glass to the sink, where she washes it out then sets it on the drying rack. A sad grimace is on her face when she looks at me. "He isn't going to reply."

My head snaps toward her. "How do you know? What's going on?"

She stares at her nails. "Robert texted me a while ago. Spider is leaving for LA. He doesn't want you."

I sit down. *No, that can't be right.* He asked me to come to LA with him. He wants me as much as I want him.

"When?"

She shrugs. "Soon."

An incoming text vibrates my phone and I pick it up, my heart soaring when I see it's from him.

I read it, and my heart drops.

I can't. Goodbye.

SEVENTEEN

Rose

B Y MONDAY, IT'S BEEN THREE days, and I haven't heard from Spider again. Somehow I've managed to keep myself from texting him or going by the penthouse. I'm angry with him for the cryptic goodbye and I'm still livid over Anne's interference. She's called me and texted me numerous times, but I refuse to answer.

I trudge along at Claremont Prep, pushing them both out of my head.

But I can't focus.

My head goes to Spider in each class, my brain and heart drunk with thoughts of his edgy, dangerous looks. The way his eyes follow me wherever I go. The way his body feels pressed against my naked skin. I want that. I want *him*.

He's on drugs.

He uses girls.

I play back all the things Anne has told me.

My heart doesn't care.

Where is he?

Why hasn't he texted me?

What did I do wrong?

As soon as the bell rings for us to head to our last period, I dodge past the onslaught of students and walk out the double front doors like I have every right to. No one notices, and I heave out a sigh of relief.

I hop in my car and drive out of Highland Park, headed toward the penthouse. I've done my best to pretend like everything is fine, like I'm not thinking about him every second, but it's a lie.

After a twenty-minute drive where I jam out to his music, I find a place to park on Bandera Avenue, a few blocks from his building. Still wearing my blue and green plaid school skirt, navy knee-high socks, and a white Peter Pan collared shirt, I jog to the park across from his place.

It's a sunny day, but a dark cloud shadows the sun and dread pools in my gut.

The air feels ominous.

I look up at the top of the building and my eyes land on the balcony. I stand there, feeling stupid and second-guessing coming all this way, half-expecting him to just know I'm here and waltz out.

But he doesn't. No one comes out to the balcony and waves at me.

If he wanted you here, he would have said so, a part of my brain reminds me, but I ignore it. *He told you goodbye.*

But I don't care.

Life is about taking chances, about saying how you feel, fuck the consequences. I mean, how will you know it's the wrong decision if you never make it in the first place?

I text him, my hands nervous and wet from sweat.

Are you still here? It feels like you are.

No response as I pace around a park bench.

Half an hour goes by and the sky darkens.

Just walk in there, I tell myself. *Ask the bellman to announce you.*

But, I don't have the nerve to go inside . . . so I wait.

If he wants to tell me goodbye, it's going to be to my face.

I type, **I'm outside your apartment and I'm not leaving until you see me.**

I groan at how needy I sound, but I think it's too late to care. I'm too far gone to care how I sound to him.

Just then a black limo pulls up to the curb and a pretty girl in her early twenties gets out wearing a pale pink mini skirt, white stiletto heels, and a soft white sweater that clings to every curve. Her brown hair is up in a ponytail and tied with a polka-dot bow.

I wonder who she is as a ping hits my phone.

Go home, Rose. I can't do this with you right now.

He is here. I knew it.

You feel something for me, I reply.

There's a twenty-second delay before he responds. I know because I'm counting, my heart racing.

No, I don't.

I feel like he's slapped me. I stumble back to the bench and watch as dog walkers pass by. Affluent women eye me carefully, and I know what they see—a schoolgirl with a phone clutched to her chest as if it's a lifeline.

I focus back on my phone.

Not buying your bullshit. There's something big between us. What's wrong with admitting it?

Five long minutes tick by as hopelessness and anger stir inside me.

God.

Why don't I just leave?

Why am I here again?

To talk to him.

To tell him goodbye to his face.

To make him tell me goodbye to my face.

He doesn't want you, Rose.

He does.

I type another text. **I have to be at work tonight, but I'm not going, not until I see you.**

Half an hour later and the air has chilled as a breeze blows. I shiver as I rub my arms.

A couple walks out of the building, the first people I've seen come out, and my senses jump to alertness. *It's him!* His hair is a beacon and my eyes drink him in, taking in the confident stride as he walks next to the girl in pink who exited the limousine earlier. The doorman is behind them, pushing a suitcase and carrying his guitar case.

From across the street, I feel his gaze brush over the area, but it doesn't stop on me.

He's ignoring me.

I jump up from my seat just as he tosses an arm around the pretty girl. Her fingers clutch the belt loops on his jeans as if she owns him, and as I watch, she smiles up at him, a bemused expression on her face.

He turns her to face him and kisses her on the lips. Her hands roam over his back, pressing him close.

I can't breathe.

My chest hurts.

My eyes get hot as tears form.

It's then that I notice other things about her. Her hair is down from the ponytail and is mussed as if hands have raked through it.

Her skirt, although it's hard to tell from here, appears to be on backward, with the slit in the front, as if it has been hastily pulled back on.

I want to rip out every single strand of her ugly brown hair.

I want to drag my nails across her face.

He . . . he . . . *fucking kissed her on the lips.*

I inhale a sharp breath, feeling winded. I press my hand to my chest to rub away the pain. I run out into the oncoming traffic and horns blow at me as I dodge the cars to get to them.

I stumble across the curb as I jog over. I know how I must look by now. My braid is coming apart and little wisps of untidy hair float around my face. I wear no makeup because I've rubbed it all off. My shirt is untucked, and my saddle oxfords are scuffed from beating them against the bench. I'm a total mess, and I don't even care.

"Rose?" he says my name as if he is surprised, but I don't think he is—even though there's an ashen look to his face.

I dart a quick glance at the girl, and she's sporting a blissed-out grin.

I want to vomit.

"You know this girl?" she asks him, her hand neatly finding his back pocket and tucking it in. A small giggle comes from her. "You have a stalker already? Kinda young, don't you think?"

"New stepsister."

Her eyebrows shoot up. "Oh."

"What do you want?" His eyes roam over me and I swallow, realizing he's never seen me in my school uniform.

For the first time with him, I feel terribly young. I clench my hands, pushing down the urge to run away.

I came all this way. I ran across four rows of traffic to get this moment.

There's no going back now.

My eyes look only at him and not at the brunette, although I know her face will forever be branded on my brain.

"I need to talk to you," I say as the driver of the limo emerges and opens the back door for them.

Spider motions to the vehicle with a flip of his hand. "I'm leaving for LA. There isn't anything left to say. Our parents took care of that."

But his body says something different. There's an anguished look on his face that matches mine, and his shoulders are stiff as he faces me head on, eating me up with his gaze. His brown eyes are locked on mine, and just like him, I refuse to let the connection be lost.

"You're lying." I'm closer now and I smell him, the scent of worn leather, cigarette smoke, and spice all mingling together to form his own particular heady scent. I want to bathe in it. I want his arms around me and not around her.

The girl—*God, I hate her*—looks up at Spider and traces a slim hand down his face. A resigned expression flits across her face as her eyes bounce from me to him. "Talk to her, babe. She needs to hear it from you. I'll be waiting in the car."

I watch as she prances past me and slides into the dark cavern of the back seat. Pretty soon, he'll be sitting back there with her. They'll be kissing again . . .

Stop.

Don't.

Fuck.

Her skirt is on backward.

I close my eyes. They were together, probably naked on his bed upstairs where I was only a few days ago.

His bloodshot gaze burns into mine, his eyes like roadmaps. He hasn't slept, or he's hungover—maybe both.

"Say what you need to say. Go off on me. I'm ready, Rose." His words are soft and tender, and I realize he needs me to lash out, but I'm not going to make this easy for him.

"I love you," I say.

His eyes flare and his lips part as a whoosh of air comes out. "Don't say that."

"Why not? It's true. I think you love me too."

He shakes his head. "You'll never hear me say those words, Rose. I don't love anyone. Love is for people who want to get hurt."

"I can't help how I feel," I cry out.

"You're infatuated with who you think I am." He points to the girl inside the limo. "You know I fucked her, right?"

Rage erupts in an instant and I shove at his shoulders, making him stumble back against the concrete pavement. "Fuck you and all the girls you fuck. You don't get to tell me how I feel."

He pales. "God . . . I'm sorry. This is what I do. I cock everything up, remember? *I'm lost*, Rose. I'm not what you need—*ever*."

I shake my head at him. "Let me come to LA with you."

He closes his eyes and opens them, pain there, yearning . . . *for me*.

I know it. I see it.

"What you're suggesting is impossible. I have a career to think about. You have college."

"I don't care." I rush through the words, hoping to convince him. "I-I know it's unexplainable but when I see you . . . I'm home, like we're pieces of a puzzle that have finally come together."

"You might want me now, but in week or a month when I get high and cheat on you . . ." His voice trails off, strained.

I tremble. My body is in fight-or-flight mode. I look at the girl in the car. "Do you care about her?"

He taps his fingers on his jeans and his eyes refuse to look at me. "I have a plane waiting for me, Rose."

"This isn't goodbye," I say, my voice cracking. "I refuse to let you leave until you tell me I mean nothing to you—*nothing!*" I shout the last words, my hands clenched.

But I'm talking to air.

He is striding toward the limo.

"If you walk away from me now . . ." I let the words hang in the air.

He knows what I mean.

He halts, his shoulders expanding as he inhales, his hand doing that tapping thing against his leg.

I pant, saying things I don't mean, saying anything as I grasp for something he might care about. "I swear to God, if you leave me here, I'll be with Trenton . . . I'll let *him* be my first. I'll never think about you again. I swear, I won't. Is that what you want?" My voice breaks.

He stands there, and I'm counting the seconds, my eyes begging him to just turn around and look at me.

His voice is low and raspy as he pushes the words out. "Tell Trenton hello for me, love."

And then he gets in the car and it pulls away slowly.

I wipe my mouth with the back of a hand that's shaking uncontrollably.

He's gone.

With . . . someone else.

I don't know how long I stand there, maybe ten minutes, maybe half an hour. The doorman comes out and checks on me, but I ignore him.

It's not until the sky opens and it begins to rain that I finally begin to see the truth as clarity arrives in bits and pieces.

I was never special to him like he was to me.

I touch my cheeks. Tears course down my face, their wetness a reminder that I've never hurt like this before . . . *never.* I feel like I'm dying of a horrible disease, as if I might waste away.

Is this what it feels like to fall in love with someone and not have it returned?

Is this what love songs are written about?

I want to scream at the top of my lungs. I want to beat my hands on the ground. I want to throw up.

I realize that people always leave, even the ones you love the most. They weasel into your life and then slink away as if nothing happened. They leave you in the wake of their destruction and gamble your heart to pursue their own ambitions.

I know what I have to do.

I'll never let him near my heart again.

PART II

Wherever a man may happen to turn, whatever a man may undertake, he will always end up by returning to the path which nature has marked out for him.

EIGHTEEN

Spider

Two years later

A HALF-HOUR BEFORE SHOW TIME at Madison Square
Garden, I'm tossing back a shot of expensive tequila as a knock
comes on my dressing room door. It's my second drink before
the show starts. I need it to get me loose, but I'm never blitzed on
stage. I made a promise to Sebastian that I wouldn't do that, and
so far I've stuck with it.

But afterward, once the music is over and the crowds have
gone . . . it's a whole new ballgame.

I'm wearing my usual outfit for a show: a pair of black skinny
jeans and a distressed gray shirt with holes ripped artfully in the
high-dollar fabric. I'm decked out in silver jewelry and the makeup
girl has already popped by to outline my eyes in black kohl.

I fling open the door, expecting Sebastian or our drummer
Rocco. Both of them are big talkers who like to chat before they
go on . . . mostly nerves. Rocco likes to shoot the shit about the

charcoal drawings I've been doing, and Sebastian likes to talk through the sets. Max, our rhythm guitar player, is a quiet guy who likes to be alone until we go on stage.

But it's neither of them. It's Rick, one of the roadies for the *Wake Up and Die* tour we're currently doing after the huge success of our latest album.

"Hiya. What's up?" I ask.

He's chewing tobacco and swishes it aside to speak. He has a slow southern drawl; I believe he's from Alabama.

"There's a girl at the back door asking to see ya."

I arch a brow. "No groupies till the show's done, mate. Just call security."

He spits in an empty water bottle. "I radioed them but can't get them on the line."

"She'll go away once the show starts," I tell him, my head already moving on to other things. I need to call Father and verify where I'm staying here in New York after the concert. Whenever I come here, I usually end up staying at one of his properties instead of a hotel. I probably should have done that by now, but we're at the end of our tour and my head is everywhere.

"She says she knows you." He's looking at me with narrowed eyes now, like he knows something I don't.

"Don't they all?"

He glances down at the new tattoo I have on the top of my left hand, a red unfurled rose. I got it last week. On my back is another rose, which I got during the first year after I left Dallas.

"She says to tell you her name is Rose."

I feel like all the air has been sucked from the room, and I cling to the side of the metal door to keep from falling.

"Did you see her? What does she look like?" My voice is thin.

He nods. "I cracked open the door, boss. She's a looker, dressed in a tight black dress and heels. Looks like your type, a brunette."

Sebastian walks up, dressed like he's ready to go in jeans and a black leather jacket. His golden mane falls around his face, and I can see he just came from having his hair blown out. He stops short at my door. "Dude, you look like you just saw a ghost. You good?" His eyes search mine.

"Good," I push out.

He eyes us carefully but keeps walking. "See you by the stage door in a few?"

I send him a nod, but I'm looking at Rick.

He continues. "Normally, I'd just ignore girls at the back door, but well, she knows your real name: Clarence."

Pure heat ignites as images of Rose fly at me . . . our kiss on the plane . . . her under me in the penthouse . . . her breath like angel's wings as it touches my skin.

The one memory I play in my head the most is her expression when she saw me with Mila.

I shove away the image of her ashen face.

Don't think about that.

Most of all, I think about the promise I made to my father when I left Dallas. I swore to him I'd leave Rose to live her life, to grow up and be the person she's meant to be. I took his half a million dollar offer and made a life for myself in LA.

Yeah, but wouldn't you like to just . . . see her?

My heart jumps at the thought.

"Boss, what do you want me to do?"

Let her in, my body screams.

She isn't seventeen anymore.

But . . .

I'm still not clean. Sure, I have good days, but I'm *not* what she needs. I have to be strong for myself before I can be strong for her.

Sebastian yells out my name. "Ten minutes. Come on, I want to run something past you."

I stare at Sebastian blankly, my head somewhere else, and he gives me an impatient look. "You coming?"

I nod and push past Rick. "Tell her you're calling the police if she doesn't leave."

I bolt for the stage, my body wired as I cover the distance between where I am and where I need to be. I run, otherwise I might just crack.

I might open that back door and let her in.

I might press my lips to hers and tell her the truth.

That she's the one I think about when I close my eyes at night.

I SNAP AWAKE AS A police siren blares through an open window.

Fuck.

Where am I?

I look around, taking in the small, cramped flat. Clothes are strewn everywhere, and the place reeks of cigarette smoke and booze. I look up and take in the popcorn ceiling, the dark water stain on the corner of the wall. It's a dump, but I've woken up in worse places.

I scrub my face, my head banging like the drums at last night's concert.

I hear a groan from the other side of the bed.

There's a naked girl next to me and her face is unrecognizable. All I see is a mass of tangled blonde hair. *Thank fuck*—I can't take any more brunettes.

I stand and stretch, my head running through what I got into after the show.

A nightclub on top of some hotel.

Snorting blow off some chick's ass in the bathroom.

I pull on my jeans and shirt, feeling like death warmed over. I have to get the hell out of here.

"Where you going?" says the girl as she props herself up against the headboard, tits hanging out. My stomach turns and I quickly look down as I push my feet into my Chucks.

"I gotta go."

"It's still early. Let's go for breakfast." She stands, and I do a double take at how tall she is.

Ah, that at least explains why I chose her.

Tall girls, brunettes, girls with green eyes—they're all Rose in my head.

I take them, because I can't have her.

She's shrugging into a silk robe as I dart to the den.

"Wait!" she calls out. "I need your number. Don't you want to call me when you come back to New York?"

Fuck no. I cringe at the thought.

There's a straw cowboy hat sitting on the back of the couch. I snatch it up and twirl it around. "Mind if I take this?"

She murmurs an okay but tells me it's a girls' hat.

I don't give a shit; I just don't want to be recognized.

"Can I see you again?" She runs her hands down my chest as I push the hat low on my head and inch closer to the door.

I ramble off an excuse, saying I'll be out of the country on tour for the next few months, and then before she can follow me, I mumble a hasty *thank you* and head out the door.

Instead of waiting for the elevator, I take the stairs. I don't even know how high up I am, but I don't care.

I need the burn.

I take the stairs two at a time until I finally burst through the door and into the New York morning. I inhale deeply, finally able to breathe. The streets are mostly quiet because it's Sunday, and I check the street signs, popping out my phone to see where I am: Bedford Street in the Greenwich Village area.

My half-awake brain figures out I'm near NYU. I pause. Rose is nearby . . . just a few blocks away. I know because she's living in one of Father's properties, and I know that because . . . well, I know everything about Rose. Father keeps me updated and I have my own people who check in on her periodically.

I'm not even aware of what my feet are doing . . . not until I'm standing outside her building near Washington Square Park.

I dart inside a Starbucks across the street to get something to drink, and an hour later, I'm sitting on a barstool facing her place when she comes out.

She is . . . everything.

Her face is a piece of art. Her movements like a sweet song.

She cranes her neck and looks down the street as if she's expecting someone. My eyes dart wildly around . . . and then I see him walking in her direction. He's waving at her, a wide smile on his handsome face.

Trenton.

I close my eyes so I don't see them together . . . even though it should come as no surprise. After all, I put her here with him. I created this fucking mess.

I can't help but open my eyes and watch them.

I need to see it. I need to see if she's moved on from me.

He reaches her, sweeps her up in his arms, and kisses her soundly.

She wraps her arms around his neck and clings to him.

As for me . . . I die.

I fucking die.

Fuck. Fuck. Fuck.

God.

I hate myself. I hate this life I have without her. I fucking hate everything.

I can't go on without her. Not anymore. I've tried for the past two years. I've pretended I'm okay . . . but I can't do it any longer.

I want to yank her out of Trenton's arms and make her love me again.

And my heart . . . it *knows* what I have to do to make that happen.

I have to get clean.

NINETEEN

Rose

Two years later

"HAPPY BIRTHDAY, SEX-AY!" OSCAR SAYS, raising his glass in a toast as we sit inside Bono's, my favorite Italian bistro and one of the hippest places in Manhattan. I also work here part-time for extra money while I attend graduate school.

I raise my shot glass at him and slam back the tequila. The room spins just a hair as I set the glass back down on the table.

I'm in the mood to celebrate.

It's September, and both of us graduated from NYU this past May. Oscar, who ended up getting that scholarship he wanted, graduated with a design degree and managed to land a coveted job at Barneys as a sales clerk, with aspirations of being a manager someday. As for me, I'm currently enrolled in the NYU graduate program, working toward my doctorate in psychology.

"If only Trenton didn't have to work," Oscar murmurs with a little pout as he straightens his dark hipster-style glasses. "But, no worries. I'll be your boyfriend tonight and will make sure you get home sober." He pushes another shot of tequila toward me, and I give him a baleful eye.

"You know what tequila does to me," I say as I inch it back to him. "I either want to fight or take off my clothes, and I don't think I'll be doing either tonight."

"Fight, fight, fight," he says, beating his hands on the table.

I laugh as I check my phone to see if Trenton's called or texted since this morning when we met for coffee. He hasn't, and it makes me frustrated. He's been working late almost every night this week.

I sigh, reminding myself how important his new job is to him. He's a portfolio manager at a small boutique firm; thankfully, his dad knew the partners from college.

"What's Mr. Businessman doing tonight?" Marge asks as she tosses back another martini. With her curly red hair and dimpled smile, she's been a good friend to me since I moved to New York four years ago to attend NYU. We still giggle about the night she got me in the bar to see the Vital Rejects.

Yes, Anne—with Robert's encouragement—agreed to send me to NYU. They have been supportive over the past four years, even allowing Oscar and I to live in one of his buildings.

Since the night of the blow up with Spider, my relationship with Anne shifted. I don't tolerate her manipulations, and she knows it. She seems to have come a long way, and I appreciate her. She's always just wanted the best for me; we just didn't agree on what that was.

Marge waves a hand in front of my face. "Hello? Are you with us?"

"Yes," I say on a little laugh. "Trenton's out with some guys from his office. They're celebrating snagging a big client today. He's making connections and all that jazz. He'll probably show up later."

Oscar arches a brow. He and Trenton have never been great friends, and I read his face like an open book. He thinks Trenton not being here is an asshole move.

"His career's important to him," I add.

Oscar shrugs, looking dapper in his slacks and blue button-up shirt with the cuffs rolled up. "He can always catch us at the club, because we are going dancing, baby girl! I'm glad you wore your dancing shoes."

Axe, the new guy in Oscar's life, glances down and whistles at my birthday gift to myself, a pair of metallic silver Christian Louboutins—from Barneys, of course.

Oscar sighs and covers his heart. "My ten percent discount is the only reason you love me."

I slap his arm. "That's not true—I only love you because you cook like a dream."

He waggles his eyebrows. "Pancakes tomorrow?"

I throw my arms around him. "I'll make the eggs—or at least I'll try."

He laughs as a text comes in for me, and I rush to look at it, thinking it's Trenton. It isn't, but I'm not too disappointed since it's Lexa wishing me a happy birthday from Atlanta. I show it to Oscar and we take a selfie to send to her. She attended Emory University after Claremont and we've drifted apart over the years. I still enjoy hearing from her though.

A few minutes later, I leave the table to go to the restroom.

A long rectangular-shaped building, the bulk of Bono's seating is near the front with a large bar area along the right wall. There's a restroom in the back along the left side, but the place is packed and I don't feel like struggling through the Saturday night crowd of singles on the prowl. Instead, I opt to hit the restrooms on the basement level, a part of the restaurant that's less urban and more comfy, usually reserved for private parties. I once met Reese Witherspoon in this section when she was celebrating wrapping up a movie in New York.

Bono's is a popular place, especially with celebrities, and considering my resume consisted of Jo's Diner in Highland Park, I was thrilled to get a position here. Luck seems to follow me everywhere in New York; it's weird. Maybe it's because I'm just so damn glad to be out of Highland Park that my positive vibes radiate out around me.

I take the stairs carefully in my heels, and I'm on the last step, just about to turn and head into the ladies' room, when I come to a complete stop.

Shock hits me, stealing my breath. It's *him*.

There's a fierce jab to my heart . . . first love always cuts the deepest.

Spider looks down at his phone, his thumb scrolling as he turns the corner to the alcove that leads into the restroom.

He hasn't seen me yet, and my eyes greedily take him in.

His hair is longer than I remember, and I watch as he pushes it off his forehead into his sweptback style, only instead of white or blue, the color is a dark brown with blond highlights. It's new and different. It's hot as hell.

My skin warms as I stare at him unabashedly, anxious for any little detail.

Wearing a maroon V-neck cashmere sweater that fits him like a glove and a pair of skinny dress slacks, he's broader in the shoulders, taller even, although I don't think that's possible.

He looks like a guy who breaks hearts every single night with just a strum of his fingers on his guitar—or a girl's skin.

I stop that kind of thinking.

Just the memory of the girl in Dallas makes me want to vomit.

He puts the phone to his ear as if he's making a call, and almost unconsciously, I step back into the dark shadow of a corner created by the recess in the staircase.

"Is the flat ready?" I hear him say.

He doesn't seem to like what he hears because he places his free palm on the wall as if to steady himself, a vulnerable look to his shoulders as he listens to whoever is talking.

"Indeed. You didn't mention that tidbit before. How the bloody hell do you expect me to stay at the same building she's—"

He stops abruptly, as if the person on the other end has cut him off. He taps his fingers against the wall as the conversation continues. I shuffle forward, straining to hear, terrified he'll turn around and see me, but I can't seem to stop myself, especially when his tone changes to a cajoling one.

I hear snippets.

"Hiya, sweets . . . see you soon . . . love . . ."

He laughs warmly.

"Tell him I'm going to bring you a puppy, love. See how Papa likes that. . . . who's your favorite big brother, Bella?" he says, plain as day, and my chest constricts.

Bella!

Of course he knows Bella, Robert and Anne's three-year-old. We both see her now and then—just never at the same time. I'll show up for Christmas and then Robert will casually mention that Spider is arriving a few days after I leave. It's weird and bizarre but I guess he just doesn't want to see me.

"Bye, sweets. I love you. Tell Papa I'll see him soon, okay? Also, tell him to lighten up on the carrots—you need more chocolate pudding." He chuckles as he tucks the phone in his pocket, his body turning toward me. I steady myself against the wall, preparing for the moment he finally sees me.

TWENTY

Spider

"I NEED TO HIT THE loo," I yell to Sebastian over the crowd as he orders another round of drinks from the downstairs bar inside Bono's. I raise my glass of ginger ale and give him a smirk. Thanks to a damn good therapist, my art, and my father who's been supportive, I've been clean for a while.

We're celebrating with the crew because next week is our last concert and once the tour is done, Sebastian and I will be jetting off to different locations. Sebastian and company will be heading back to LA, where I used to live but have long since abandoned for a flat in London. It's less hectic there, and it feels like home.

He gives me a chin nod and I take off, needing some distance from the noise so I can call Father. He's tried to call me several times today, and this is the first opportunity I've had to get back to him.

I call and he tells me the location of my new place in the city. My head spins when he lets me know it's the same building and the same floor where Rose lives. I'm not prepared yet to see her, but there's little he can do. He doesn't have anything else available, and the personal penthouse he owns on Park Avenue is currently being painted. I could get a hotel, but groupies always find a way in, and it's loud when people walk up and down the halls at all hours of the day and night. I need peace and quiet. I need my own space.

So, I'm stuck in Greenwich Village.

Robert puts Bella on and I chat with her before I go. I tell them both goodbye and hang up the phone. I straighten up, about to head into the loo, when a shadowy female figure catches my eye under the staircase. I narrow my eyes as she ducks her head, a curtain of long auburn hair shadowing her face.

Feeling like I must be blocking the way, I immediately mutter an apology and give her room to pass.

She doesn't pass.

I look at her again, this time with more discernment, trying to get a read on her features.

Is she a stalker? Reporter? Groupie?

I study her as she takes a tentative step out from the alcove. A sense of familiarity pricks at me.

Ruby red lips.

Long legs.

A short dress.

I swallow, my chest expanding as I inch in closer.

It can't be. She isn't supposed to be working tonight. I called earlier and checked with the manager to make sure.

It's funny why I chose this place for our group tonight. It's because I want to be where she's been—without actually seeing her.

"Rose?"

Her name on my lips is like a blow to my heart.

"Spider." She moves fully out from the shadows and the

overhead lighting illuminates her face.

I suck in a sharp breath.

She's different with the auburn hair. God, I can barely believe it's her.

But it is . . .

She's beautiful . . . magnified by a million.

Wearing a short beaded white dress with spaghetti straps, she stands there with a slight tilt to her chin, as if preparing to battle. Green eyes that once read my soul peer up at me. She reaches out to steady herself on the painted white brick of the wall.

I can barely breathe, and I don't think she's unaffected by me.

"What are you doing?" I ask. *Such a stupid question.*

Her mouth opens, but nothing comes out, until finally she clears her throat. "I work here . . . literally I'm a server." Her breath and voice seem to gather strength as she speaks, her features settling into a cool mask as she composes herself.

Of course, I know this, but I can't tell her how.

I clutch both my hands in my hair, just to stop myself from reaching out to her. I mean, it's been my intention since I got clean to get her back, but I've been waiting . . . I don't know what for. God, I'm scared.

I'm fucking terrified she'll hate me.

I'm fucking terrified she'll love me and then leave me.

I'm not prepared to see her tonight, and my heart pounds.

"You're real then?"

I ask because there are nights when I think she is with me, nights when I was stoned or high and she was fuzzy image in the background.

"I am."

I lean my shoulder against the wall, digging deep for some

nonchalance. I'm fresh from a performance and feeling edgy; there's no telling what I might say to her. "I've imagined this a thousand times . . . seeing you again."

She flushes, the red color rising up her cheeks. "Yeah, I bet," she says dryly. "I came to see you at a concert two years ago. I showed up at the stage door, but you obviously didn't want to see me. It was a weak moment on my part. It'll never happen again." She shrugs. "You never manage to see me at the family holiday dinners either."

Because it hurts to see what I lost.

Someone brushes past us as they exit the restroom, and I barely look at them.

I bite my lip. "I know. I'm busy. I go home when I can. Bella . . . she's amazing. I'm crazy about her. She calls me "Spidie"."

She nods, her lips flattening.

Fuck.

She's angry with me.

Can you blame her?

She moves her head and a copper curl slides over her shoulder and down into the cleavage of her dress.

"I like your hair."

Still stupid, Spider.

She swallows. "I . . . need to go. Oscar is upstairs . . ." Her voice trails off as she turns to leave.

I grab her arm. "Wait."

"What?" She blinks down at my arm and then back up at me, swaying on her feet.

"Are you okay?"

She shakes her head, her eyes bright. "No . . . yes . . . I don't know. I just didn't expect to see you."

My heart hammers. *Fuck.* She's so . . . *Rose* . . . and my head is all over the place. "Are you glad you did?"

"No."

"Rose!" Someone calls out her name. She turns her head and her face fills with something that looks like relief.

I turn to watch as Trenton approaches, wearing a gray suit, no longer a fresh young boy of seventeen. He kisses her on the cheek before whispering something in her ear that makes her smile.

My heart flops around like a dying fish.

"Trenton, you remember my stepbrother, Spider?" She gives me a brief and rather formal smile.

He grabs my hand, shaking it firmly, looking every inch the polished businessman he clearly strives to be. More gregarious than I recall, he slaps me on the shoulder, and I notice he's been drinking, a lot, if the intensity of the smell of bourbon is anything to go by.

"Of course, the music guy. Hope you're not here to steal my girl from me." He laughs and glances at Rose, who attempts a half-smile. "She's always listening to your music, man. Loves it."

"He's my stepbrother," she murmurs.

Trenton waves her off with a grin. "You know what I mean, sweetie." He palms her lower back, just skirting her ass, and kisses her again, this time on the lips. *Shit, am I supposed to leave? Walk away?*

I can't.

It's like a train wreck you can't help but watch even though you're standing right there on the fucking tracks, knowing it's going to kill you.

"Someone's been drinking tequila," he murmurs, laughing under his breath as he curls an arm around her waist. "I know what that means. You feel like getting out of here and going back to your place sooner rather than later?"

A ghost of a smile appears on her lips. "We have clubbing plans."

He leans in to smell her neck. "You smell so fucking good."

I recall her smell, honey and vanilla. I feel my teeth grinding, but still I can't do the gentlemanly thing and leave. Instead, I clench my fists, a muscle popping in my jaw.

Trenton eases back and sends me a sly look. "Sorry for the PDA. I haven't seen her much this week . . ." he rambles, something about an important job and how he hated to miss her birthday celebration so he tore himself away to see her . . . *blah, blah, blah.*

I'm not listening. I'm watching her.

She stands in the circle of his arms, and we stare at each other.

It's as if Trenton doesn't exist and we're silently having our own conversation.

She appears cool, like a fucking mannequin in a department store, but I know it's a lie when I see the telltale pulse in her neck, the way it throbs furiously against her creamy skin.

She breaks eye contact with me to smile up at Trenton and I exhale, feeling angry. *Look at me!* I want to say.

Fuck.

Four years is a long time. A lot of things can happen—the Olympics, the World Cup, an entire presidential term.

Hell, anything can happen.

Maybe she's completely over me.

I'm not over her.

"Hey, Oscar and some friends are upstairs," Trenton says, his words penetrating my brain and bringing me out of my fog. "You wanna join us?" He's looking at me.

"I can't, gotta rest up." I palm my spider tattoo, a sure sign

I'm in a tailspin, and Rose watches me, her analytical brain not missing it. A frown appears on her face as she intently stares, her eyes focused on my hand on my neck.

Shit.

I quickly remove my hand and stick it in my pocket.

Her eyes snap back up to mine as she sucks in a sharp breath, her top teeth digging into her bottom lip. She isn't fooled. She sees the rose tattoo on the top of my hand.

"Oh," Trenton says, frowning. "But you guys haven't seen each other in a while, and it's her birthday . . ."

"I'm sure he's here with other people," Rose says quietly.

I nod, grabbing on to that. "Yeah, the whole band is here— roadies too. We're in town for one more concert and then I'm off to London." I clear my throat, my eyes eating her up one last time. "Look, it's been great to see you . . . both of you."

I don't even give them time to murmur their goodbyes before I'm bolting away and back into the bar area. I find Sebastian, send him a final salute, and head out into the night.

I WAKE UP COLD AND lonely in a king-sized bed and glare at the sliver of sunlight that glints in from the glass door that leads to the balcony outside. Scratching at the scruff on my jawline, I stretch out, loosening muscles that are tight from being on tour for the past four months. Besides the concert, the one thing I'm looking forward to the most before I leave New York is my art show. It's been part of my recovery therapy and seeing it come to life means a lot to me.

The sound of music comes from the neighboring flat, and I

turn my face toward the wall, listening. It's one of ours, a remake of Pat Benatar's "Love is a Battlefield". I'm on backup, and the guitar is spot on.

A small smile plays around my mouth.

It's surreal to think about how much success we've had, a lot of it owing to my father's money and influence.

Thinking of him brings back everything from last night, and suddenly, I'm wide awake and standing.

Only one thought is running through my head right now.

I place my palm on the wall where the music came from.

Is that her?

Father said she was on the same floor as me and there's only four apartments per level. I inhale a deep breath, as if I can smell her scent.

She is *here* . . . right here.

I fucking know it.

For the first time in a long time, unadulterated and unfettered joy that has nothing to do with drugs takes me over.

I sink down on the bed, feeling lightheaded.

She's so close.

The question is . . . what am I going to do about it?

TWENTY-ONE

Rose

MY MUSIC BLARES FROM MY alarm at eight in the morning, my cue to get my butt out of bed. It's Sunday and I have the eleven o'clock brunch shift at Bono's.

My head pounds and my stomach rolls as I sit up. I definitely shouldn't have had that last shot. *Ugh.* I scratch at the rat's nest that is my hair and let out a deep exhale.

I hear Oscar banging pots and pans around as he makes his usual Sunday breakfast for us. From the bathroom, the sound of water comes on, and I figure it's Trenton already up. He lives a few blocks from here, but stays over sometimes, or I stay at his place. He's been asking me to move in with him permanently since graduation, but something holds me back. Besides, Robert lets Oscar and I live here rent-free. It's not over-the-top fancy, but it's nice and in a great part of Greenwich Village.

Oscar breezes in carrying a large ceramic unicorn mug with *I'm Magical* written on it. "Morning, sunshine. Thought you might need one of these after seeing a certain someone last night." He sits next to me on the bed, sipping from his own matching mug.

I try to grin, as much as I can with a hangover. "Remind me to never drink again."

He arches a brow. "You know what Frank Sinatra says about people who don't drink . . . that when they wake up in the morning, it's sad, because that's as good as they're going to feel all day." He chuckles as he sips on his coffee.

I smirk. "Your hero is wise, and you're an old soul with the heart of a hipster."

"You know it." He eyes me carefully. "Seriously though, do you recall everything that happened last night?"

I squint, my brain attempting to retrace my night after seeing Spider, but it's blurry. I scrunch my nose up. "Did I order something called a Cherry Blow Pop?"

"Three of them."

I almost gag. "That's why I'm so queasy."

He crosses his legs. "Not surprising with peach and amaretto liqueur, and some kind of green liquid that I have no idea what it was."

"That's not even cherry!"

"I distinctly recall you not caring as long as it did the job." He cocks his head. "But . . . a word of advice: the things you say when you're drunk are usually what you really think when you're sober."

My head throbs even harder, if possible. "Crap. What did I say?"

Oscar grimaces. "You went on a tiny rant about sexy rock stars and how they're all assholes who screw anything with a pulse."

I bite my lip. "Crap. Did I mention you-know-who?"

He gives me a look. "Baby girl, pretty sure we all knew

who—even Trenton."

I curse under my breath. Four years ago when I started dating Trenton, I didn't bring up Spider. At first it was because I didn't want Trenton to think he was my rebound guy when he so obviously was, and then later when my feelings for Trenton had grown into love, it just wasn't appropriate. Spider *is* my stepbrother, and most think it's wrong—especially people from Highland Park.

"Thanks for the warning," I say as I take a deep pull of the frothy liquid and lean my head against the headboard. "What would I do without you?"

"You'd be considerably less stylish, and you'd be hungry."

I grin. "I'd have more money though."

"Who needs money when you have me?"

The water clicks off in the bathroom and I stand, noticing I'm still wearing my underclothes from last night's outfit: a white lace bra and panty set. I sigh. No sex with Trenton; unfortunately, I'm not surprised. Lately, we seem to be drifting, both of us caught up in our everyday lives. But I do love him and I know he loves me.

Oscar whistles his appreciation. "Your body is rocking, but word of advice, your hair is ready for Halloween." He pats me on the leg. "Now hop on up and let Mama Oscar make you some pancakes."

"I love you!" I call to his back as he flounces out of my room and heads into the kitchen.

By the time Trenton makes it out of the bathroom, I'm dressed in a pair of yoga pants and a camisole. I'll wait to shower after breakfast; my topsy-turvy belly needs grease to make it feel better, and quick.

He comes into my bedroom already dressed in madras shorts and a sports polo. I study his face, looking for signs that I revealed too much about Spider the night before, but he seems his usual calm self. A bit unemotional, nothing seems to ruffle his feathers. Sometimes I wish he had more passion, but it's just . . . him. At least he's predicable.

I recall the night we first slept together. It was after Spring Fling and my heart was still devastated from Spider. Lonely and depressed, I did what I told Spider I'd do; I focused on Trenton. That night, Trenton got us a hotel room and was gentle and sweet when he took me. Lying in his arms, I cried for my stupid broken heart, but in the coming days, I learned to love him. We've been together ever since, an easy and drama free relationship.

He gives me a peck on the lips, smelling minty and fresh.

"Where you headed?" I ask. "I thought we'd eat breakfast together."

He styles his hair in front of a mirror propped on my dresser, working product into his sandy blond locks. "Can't. I'm meeting some of the partners at a country club in Connecticut. I need to get on the road if I want to make tee time."

I'm disappointed, but also relieved.

I need some space today to think, to rehash every detail of my interaction with Spider last night—which is wrong. I shouldn't even be thinking about him. "It feels like we barely see each other these days."

His eyes find mine in the mirror. "They like me, and I need to foster these relationships if I want to move up. I have a good feeling about this company." He walks over and wraps me in a hug. "Come on, don't be glum. You know, you don't have to wait tables or even get your graduate degree—"

"But I want to," I say, cutting him off.

His mouth tightens. "It just feels like between you working

at Bono's and school, you're too busy for me."

I stiffen and pull away. This is a familiar argument with us since graduation. He's a traditional guy who wants me to be done with school and spend my time with him. Sometimes it feels like he's putting distance between us and staying busy on purpose, just to manipulate me into doing what he wants—which is to quit everything and move in with him.

He exhales. "Then maybe we can do lunch one day this week?"

"Of course."

He heads to my bedroom door, but before he goes, he looks back at me, a quizzical expression on his face. "By the way, I find it curious that Spider didn't want to celebrate with us last night. Is there some kind of tension between you two?"

"No," I say rather quickly.

He frowns. "You sure? You ranted about rock stars last night. There seemed to be some . . . animosity there."

"I was trashed. There's no telling what I said." I wave him off. "Spider's . . . fine. We just lead very different lives."

He nods slowly, but there's a look in his eyes that says he doesn't believe me. He pauses for a few moments as if he's going to say something else, but then he walks out the door. I let out a sigh of relief when I hear him telling Oscar goodbye in the kitchen as he leaves.

Half an hour later, things are looking up as I stuff a wad of the best bacon I've ever had into my mouth. Then a knock sounds at the door.

Oscar is busy frying *more* bacon, so I saunter over to the door and open it, half-expecting to see Trenton. He's forever leaving stuff here and then making a mad dash to find it.

It isn't Trenton.

"Morning, stepsister."

Shock ripples over me as my hand grips the edge of the door, and just like that, I can't breathe. He's in front of me—again. I will my heart to slow down.

He seems more confident this morning, and it throws me.

"What . . . how did you get here?"

He gives me that devil-may-care shrug of his. "I'm your neighbor. Right next door."

"That doesn't make sense." I can't think straight. I can't even begin to connect the dots. He's entirely too handsome for how early in the morning it is, and I know I look like a deranged person with scary hair.

"Because my father is your stepfather and he owns this building. He told me last night we were on the same floor. I heard your music this morning, and I just made a guess that this one was yours. Guess I was right." He leans back and points to the apartment door to my left. "That one's mine."

"Oh." I exhale, brushing at my hair. "Have you always stayed at 4E when you're in town?" I know exactly how many concerts he's had in New York—three. I went to the one where he didn't come out to see me, but I push that out of my head.

He shakes his head. "Father said this was all he had in town—"

Oscar yells from the kitchen, cutting him off. "Good grief, stop grilling the man and let him come in and eat! We're from Texas, girl—where's your hospitality?"

I smirk. I guess Oscar heard everything we said.

Interest lights Spider's eyes. "That would be great," he says softly. "It smells great in here, to be honest. Plus, I don't have any coffee over there. I'm dying."

Screw southern hospitality. I want to tell him to go fuck

himself, I really do, but I can't. It's *him* in the flesh, and he has a power over me.

"May I come in, Rose?" His eyes are pools of sunlight through amber, and I sigh.

"I'd never deny a man coffee." I grit my teeth and step aside to let him in, and his hand accidentally brushes against mine. Electricity hums, igniting my insides, but I shake it off.

He enters the kitchen and I make mean eyes at Oscar for inviting him, but Oscar barely notices. He's giving Spider air kisses on both cheeks like they're old friends. I stick my tongue out at him behind Spider's back, and he ignores me.

"What will it be this morning, Spiderman? Pancakes? Omelet? Mind you, you better eat good, because I only do this once a week."

Spider grins as he makes his way to the counter to pour himself a cup of coffee. "I'll take anything you have left."

"You're awfully chipper this morning," I grumble.

He sips at his mug. "Clean living. It's amazing how great mornings are when you're not recovering from a bender."

I give him a look, searching his face for truth. Robert mentioned that Spider was clean the last time I went to visit them, but I refused to think on it too much, to wonder about what his life was like now.

He pauses. "I haven't used alcohol or drugs in almost two years. Now cigarettes . . . that's another story."

"That's incredible. I'm really happy for you. Congratulations."

He shrugs and gets quiet.

Thankfully, the silence is filled when Oscar sets a plate down in front of him. Spider dives in, slicing his meal and eating it with excruciating slowness, savoring each bite.

He looks hot—just eating—and it drives me insane. I huff and tear into a piece of pancake, probably looking like a mangy dog.

A bit later, Oscar gets up to put his mug in the sink. "Well, lovebirds, I hate to go, but I've got to go check on my man. Can I count on you two to get along while I'm gone?"

I sputter. "Of course."

Spider grins. "Thanks for letting me crash your breakfast."

Oscar gives Spider a serious look. "No problem. Just don't be hurting my girl again . . . or I will kill you." Before either of us can reply, he's darting to his bedroom and shutting the door.

I inhale, mortified as Spider looks at me, his eyes dark with an emotion I can't read. Maybe I don't want to read it.

He wipes his mouth, his gaze intently studying me. "Do you want me to leave? I'm assuming you only asked me in because of Oscar."

I swallow, my chest hurting as I take in his chiseled face, the way his perfectly sculpted cheekbones accentuate his jawline. My fingers ache to brush his hair off his face. *Fuck.* He's ripping my heart open all over again . . . just by sitting in front of me. "Yes."

He nods, a look of understanding on his face as he stands.

I stand with him, my hand clenching as I speak the words my brain couldn't form last night. "The truth is, I don't want to see you again. What you did to me . . . how you hurt me . . . it can never be undone. I just want to forget it ever happened, but I can't do that when I see you."

He nods. "Before I do, there's something I want you to know."

"What?"

He sighs and opens his mouth, but nothing comes out. He bites his lip and rakes a hand through his hair then rubs at the scruff on his jaw. He's fumbling, trying to find the words, but he can't.

My eyes go to the rose tattoo I saw last night, on the top of the hand with *LOST* on the knuckles. "Is that about me?"

He looks down at it. "Yeah. I get one"—he takes a deep breath—"every year we're apart."

I don't believe him. My face feels hot.

He exhales. "The first year, I got a rose on my back. The hand was next." He pushes up the sleeve on his navy sweater and shows me the inside of his arm, where my name is written in tiny script along his bicep. "I got this on year three."

I take deep breaths, processing his words.

He stands there, fidgeting.

"And this year? What did you get?"

"Nothing. I'm waiting . . ."

"For what?" I say, my voice shaky, and I want to yank it back. I don't want him to see how his words are affecting me, how his vulnerability is tugging at me.

He bites his lip and looks at me long and hard. "For you. This is the year I get you back."

I gasp and take a step back. "You have no right to assume that—*no right*."

"I know."

"I have a life without you—a perfect one."

"I know." He sticks his hands in his skinny jeans.

"I'm with Trenton—"

"Trust me, I know."

"And you can't expect to just waltz in here and pick back up—

"I don't."

"You hurt me!" I yell at him, tired of his calm. I need him to be just as angry as I am. "You slept with someone else immediately after almost sleeping with me! You left me in Dallas after you promised you'd take me to LA. You're a liar, a horrible, horrible liar, and I hate you for it." My words are bitter and harsh, and it feels good to get them out, to say all the things that have built up inside me since he left.

He swallows, his face working with emotion, looking conflicted. "It's just . . . I knew what kind of girl you were, tough and strong. I knew if you really wanted me, you'd find a way, and I couldn't let that happen. That's why I hurt you, Rose." His voice sounds as if it's been dragged over gravel. "I . . . I promised Father I'd leave you alone."

"But why?"

He faces me head on, his face like stone. "He gave me a half a million dollars to leave Dallas and start my career. The condition was I had to leave you behind."

I close my eyes. "And look at you now . . . you're famous."

He shakes his head. "No, Rose, look at *you*."

"What do you mean?"

"You graduated NYU summa cum laude. You're in graduate school. You're living the life you wanted."

Tears prick my eyes at the idea that he knows things about me that I've never told him, as if he's kept up with me . . . but I hurriedly blink them away. I can't be soft around him. It hurts too much. "You have no right to assume I wouldn't have had those things with you in LA. You made the decision to take that money *for you* because you realized I wasn't worth the trouble. I would have just gotten in the way of the things you really wanted to do—fucking anything that moved, coke up your nose, whatever."

His face pales. "I deserve that. I left you with no explanation, and that wasn't right. I'm sorry for Dallas. I wasn't the man you needed."

"You think you are now?" Disbelief is evident in my tone as

I glare at him.

Who does he think he is?

Does he think he can just stroll right back into my life as if the past four years didn't even happen?

He studies me carefully, his gaze brushing over my face and lingering on my lips. "You're mine, Rose, always will be."

And then he's gone before I can even form a response.

TWENTY-TWO

Rose

IT'S WEDNESDAY NIGHT WHEN I snap awake at the sound of thunder rolling across the tall buildings in Manhattan.

Perfect, just what I need—and on a night when Oscar is staying over with Axe.

I check my phone and see that it's one in the morning and actually Thursday. *Ugh.* I clamber out of bed in the darkness and make my way to the bathroom. It's been a weird week and has everything to do with Spider and his *you're mine, Rose* comment on Sunday.

I stare at myself in the mirror, seeing the dark circles from the lack of sleep this week.

Just then a bolt of lightning flashes across the sky and the strike reverberates through the concrete walls in my apartment. A scream escapes me as the power goes out, plunging me into total darkness. I hate storms since the night Mama was killed.

Stumbling around in the dark, I make my way back to my

bedroom, where I promptly stub my toe and yelp. *Dammit!* Hopping on one foot and cursing, I manage to find the nightstand drawer where I keep my little flashlight in case of the zombie apocalypse . . . or a blackout.

But, it's not there. *Oscar.* He went on a camping trip last month with Axe and asked to borrow it. I yell at him in my head.

Fumbling around on my pillows, I find my phone and use the flashlight on it, but I know it won't last long since my battery is low. Walking to the balcony door, I gather the nerve to peek out, trying to ignore the harsh boom from another strike of lightning. Blackness for a city block meets my gaze. No red lights, no storefront lights, no streetlights, nothing. The lightning must have hit a transformer somewhere.

It's eerie in the city, and I shiver again.

Candles. I need candles.

I'm in the kitchen, rummaging through drawers in search of Oscar's supply of scented candles from Bath & Body Works and matches. I'm not having any luck and when I bump my head on an open cabinet door, I curse a blue streak.

To make matters worse, all I find are candles and no matches. Aggravated and fighting a freak-out, I decide to just forget it and go huddle under the blankets on my bed while praying for the storm to pass soon.

A knock sounds at the door, and I yelp.

"Rose? Are you okay?"

I hobble to the door and crack it open, leaving the latch on. I blare my phone light at him, making him squint.

Wearing nothing but a pair of Union Jack boxers is Spider. His muscled abs are on display, and it's clear he's bulked up since I last saw him. His chest is broad and sculpted, his biceps look like

I could bounce a quarter off them, and the deep V at his waist is making me salivate. *All hail, England.*

I move the light down to check out his legs. Yep, they're sexy too. *Dammit.*

I tear my eyes off his body and focus on his face.

At least his hair is sticking straight up. *Serves him right.*

He holds his hand up to block the light in his eyes. "Can you please turn that thing off? You're blinding me."

He looks past me and into the foyer area. "I heard you scream and got worried. I remembered that storms scare you."

"How did you know that?" I ask, not recalling ever telling him.

"When we met on the plane, you told me."

"Oh." I bit my lip, surprised he remembered. I recall another tidbit from the plane. "Are you still scared of Dolly Parton hiding in your shower?"

A grin curls his lips. "Fucking terrified."

Lightning strikes again, and I flinch.

"Are you okay? Do you need anything?"

I stand there and mean to tell him I'm fine, but something in me softens.

"Oscar stole my flashlight and I don't have any matches," I say with a smirk.

He grins and holds up a small flashlight. "Want some company?"

A small battle rages inside me. I'm uncomfortable with the tension between us, but I also hate being alone during storms.

I exhale, remove the latch, and take a step aside so he can enter.

My insides quake at our close proximity, especially since I can see all his rippling muscles and tousled hair.

I eye his boxers. "Aren't you cold?"

His lips quirk. "Want me to put some pants on?"

Thunder rolls again and a bolt of lightning strikes, a bright flash coming in from the windows at the back of the apartment. It illuminates the foyer and den area for a few seconds. My hands clench. "No," I say hurriedly. "Don't leave me. Not until the storm is over. This lightning . . . it drives me nuts."

His brow furrows, his gaze taking in how I'm leaning against the entry table. "Hey, I'm here. I'm not going anywhere." He shines his light around the apartment, checking out the big windows at the back.

"Do you have windows in your bedroom?"

I nod. "Floor-to-ceiling on one side. I've thought about asking Robert for some kind of window treatment, but he's done so much . . ." My voice trails off. "The only rooms that don't have windows are the bathrooms and the kitchen area."

He thinks for a moment and says. "Come on, I have an idea."

I follow him as he marches into the den and considers my furniture. Seeming to come to a decision, he begins to move them around. My brow wrinkles as I watch him push a chair over to the sectional. He grabs a floor lamp and moves it close to the chair. *What is he doing?*

He leans over to get a better look at an end table and I sigh. His tight ass . . . I close my eyes, my body warming. I'm getting hot, and it isn't from the humidity of the storm.

"Where's Oscar?" he asks as he shifts the coffee table.

I bite my lip. "He's staying at Axe's tonight."

"Ah."

I can't wait any longer, baffled by his actions. "What are you doing? Some kind of feng shui?"

He tosses me a grin, and for the first time since seeing him, it feels like it used to with us . . . like home.

"You'll see, love."

I follow him as he makes his way unerringly into my bedroom, removes the pillows and sheets, and then carries them back into the den, still using the flashlight to light the way.

"I need some more quilts. Do you have any?"

I nod and show him the linen closet. He grabs an armful and goes back into the den.

He arranges the quilts and pillows on the carpet then drapes several sheets over the furniture he's moved in closer to the center of the room. The floor lamp is the highest point and creates a tent effect. He pats the floor, indicating a small opening he's made for me to crawl through.

"You made a fort," I say. "For me to hide in?"

He nods, doing one of those effortless shrugs. "Just want you to feel safe. At least the lightning won't be as noticeable. I mean, I know you can still see through the sheets—"

"It's perfect," I say, chewing on my lip. "Are you coming in?"

"If you want me to?" There's a hesitant sound in his voice.

"I do."

I lean over and crawl through and glance over my shoulder to see him watching me, probably taking in the yellow lace underwear I'm wearing under my roomy t-shirt.

Once I get settled, he tosses me the flashlight. "Now close your eyes and count to a hundred—out loud, so I can hear you. I'll be right back."

My eyes flare as he stands up. "You're leaving?"

"Just for a second. Hang on—" and then he's gone. I hear him opening my front door and then silence.

I sigh, close my eyes, and begin to count.

He arrives back at around the seventy mark. I hear him scuf-fling around my den, a loud grunt when he bumps into something, and then the flick of a lighter.

The opening of the fort door rustles as he comes inside, but I keep my eyes closed. His shoulder brushes against mine, and his voice is hushed. "Okay, you can open your eyes now."

I open them and my focus is transfixed on the myriad of can-dles he set up around the room and lit. Several are on the mantel, and a few are on the foyer table next to the front door.

My chest expands, and I find that I can't look at him. "It's . . . a wonderland."

He squeezes my shoulder, both of us sitting cross-legged on the quilts. "The next time you have a storm, do this instead. Maybe it will change your whole perspective."

"Yes." I don't know what else to say.

I'm overwhelmed by him. By his thoughtfulness.

He turns my chin toward him, and . . . we're so close. I see that he's put on pajama pants after all; they're a blue and green plaid and hang loosely from his hips.

"Are you still scared?"

"No," I whisper. I'm something else entirely.

He pulls something out from behind him, a small package wrapped in thick, expensive paper and tied with a burlap bow.

"What's this?" My voice is soft and a bit breathless.

"A gift. I . . . I've had it for a while."

"Why didn't you send it to me?"

A long sigh comes from him and he swallows. "Rose . . . I couldn't see you or have any contact with you . . . not until I was clean. That's why I didn't come to the back door the night of the concert."

I process his words, feeling them out. "You've been clean for a while, right? If it was so important to you . . . why haven't you seen me?"

He rubs a hand over his face. "I don't know . . . being clean has been hard and I'm figuring it out as I go. I see a therapist and I draw to keep the demons away. Father and I . . . we talk more and try to see each other often. Just having his support . . . it means a lot to me."

I nod.

He chews on his bottom lip. "There hasn't been one day that goes by that I haven't wondered how you are and what you're doing." He stops and inhales a deep breath. "I got clean for you. For us."

"There is no us," I remind him.

"Yet."

His words send a wave of pure need through me, but I squash it down.

He hurt you, Rose, I remind myself.

I take the package from him and open it gently. My eyes water when I see what it is—a first edition copy of *Jane Eyre*—and I look up at him. "This must have cost you . . . thousands."

I flip the book jacket over, tracing my fingers over the carefully preserved title page.

He shrugs, his face soft.

I stare down at the brown cover, my hands clutching it like a lifeline. I never want to let it go. He kisses me gently on the cheek and suddenly I can't breathe, my whole body warm and tingling.

He fingers a lock of my hair. "I finished it, you know, a long time ago."

"What did you think?" I ask.

"At the core, it's a story about destiny, Jane's destiny, and how it's intertwined with Rochester's. Fate's a wonderful thing, right?" A small laugh escapes him, and I wonder if he's thinking what I am . . . that fate brought us together that day at the Quickie Mart and then later on the airplane.

He continues. "Jane's a fucking boss, like you, even though people want to bring her down. She just wants . . . I don't know, freedom to be her own person and make her own decisions."

"Yes."

He clears his throat, his lips closer to mine than before, the change in our position almost imperceptible. "She turns down Rochester's offer of being his mistress because she wants to be true to herself."

"What about Rivers?" I ask, inquiring about Jane's other love interest. "What do you think of him?"

He laughs softly. "He's a religious wanker."

I'm so entirely fascinated by his words . . . the fact that he read it because of *me*.

"How do you know she doesn't love the wanker?" I say, my eyes boring into his.

"Because she can't forget Rochester. She'll never be over him, and when she hears his voice calling for her, she goes . . ." His voice stops, his face flushing as he cups my cheek.

His mouth halts a few inches from mine, his chest rising and falling rapidly.

If I don't touch him . . .

God, if I don't touch him . . . I'm going to die right here.

"Rose, I really want to kiss you right now."

"God, yes," I say breathlessly.

TWENTY-THREE

Spider

I KISS HER SOFTLY, AS if we're on a first date, tasting her with reverence, my lips claiming hers so excruciatingly slow, as if saying, *You can pull away at any time.*

I don't want to scare her.

My emotions are incredibly fierce at this moment, hot with need, and I have to hold myself back from crushing her in my arms.

I breathe her in, my hand encircling her neck and tugging her closer, until all I can think, smell, want is her.

"Spider," she whispers between small kisses down my neck, her teeth scraping across my collarbone, making me hiss, my cock already hard as steel.

I groan, my hand slipping under her shirt and palming her breast, my fingers tweaking her nipple.

"We shouldn't," she says as I raise her shirt up to her shoulders.

I tilt her chin up and stare into her eyes. "There's nothing wrong with the way I feel about you and how I think you feel about me, but this is your decision. I want you. I want you so much that I can't breathe."

She closes her eyes, her lashes fluttering against her cheeks.

"Look at me."

Her eyes open.

"Just tell me to stop and I will." My thumb runs across her lower lip. "You say the word and I'll never kiss these lips again. We can go on pretending and tiptoeing around each other when we both fucking know that this heat between us is something we can't ignore forever. Fate has other plans. She wants this. Do you want it?"

A slow blush starts up her neck. "Yes."

My hand winds in her hair and I tug her face back to mine. "Then let me show you how much I want you."

I kiss her again, harder this time, my teeth and tongue owning hers.

She pants, one hand threading through my hair to grasp my skull, tugging on me while her other pulls at my pajama bottoms, slipping inside and underneath my silk boxers to grasp my cock.

I ease away from her with a small laugh and lay her back against the pillows, my eyes devouring her. "You're gonna make me blow too soon, love."

"That's okay. We can always go again." She shimmies out of her shirt and kicks her panties off, making me groan.

She's in a hurry, and I suspect it's because, like me, she's in the moment and afraid of this thing between us disappearing.

Tall and toned with perfectly sized breasts that make my mouth water, she's the epitome of the female form in my eyes. She always has been.

I shove down my pants and boxers and kick them out of the way.

Her eyes go right to the rod that's straight up.

"I know, it's formidable."

She giggles.

"What's so funny?" I say, looking down at it.

"Nothing. It's just . . . I've waited so long, and I'm nervous . . ." Her voice trails off.

I reach down and palm her head, kissing her. "Me too. I feel like a teenager with you."

She leans over and takes me into her mouth, her hand pumping my shaft as she explores me with long licks, pushing down with her lips until I feel the tightness of her throat.

I toss my head back, not prepared as she works me over, sending my heart into overtime as she sucks me off. "Fuck . . . Rose."

She moans, humming against me, and I let her suck me down a few more times before I pull away.

I want to taste her . . . be inside her.

I ease her back to the quilt and kiss her again. She cranes upward, wanting more as I move down her body, not stopping until she's spread out in front of me. My lips explore her, the bend in her knee, the curve of her hips, the slope of her neck. Part of me wants to take her hard because it feels like I've waited forever, but the other side of me wants to be gentle. I don't know which one is going to win.

I roll her over to her side and pay special attention to the tattoo at the top of her back, the one with my old number inside the butterfly. My tongue traces the outline, my lips brushing across her satin skin. Working my way around to her hip, my fingers slip inside her slit and finger her.

"You're fucking wet, love."

She moans as my mouth follows, tasting her. She calls my

name and parts her legs wide, arching closer as I strum her, reaching for her G-Spot.

"You like?" I say against her center, my tongue toying with her clit.

"Don't stop," she murmurs, a hitch in her voice.

I can never deny her anything. I pulse my tongue over her, taking her nub and sucking hard as she screams my name and breaks apart, her walls clenching around the two fingers I have inside her.

She falls back against the pillows. "No one's ever done that."

My eyes flare, and *fuck*, I don't want to say his name, but a million questions burn in my mind.

She looks down, obviously embarrassed. "I never wanted him to."

I shove thoughts of him away and focus on her.

"We got a lot more to go." I grin. "Do you have condoms?"

She nods and tells me where they are then I dash to get them. In ten seconds, I'm back inside the fort and her arms are open. "Took you long enough."

I laugh and ease between her legs then flip us over, rolling her on top of me.

"What are you doing?" she says softly.

"This." I spread her apart with my thumbs and seat her on my cock, groaning at the feel of her tightness against my dick as I slide inside. Yes. This.

She moans and arches her back as I hang on to her hips and pump. Her tits bounce with each thrust, nipples straining toward me, and I divide my lips between them, my tongue tasting her sweat, my nose inhaling her skin.

She's beautiful.

She's everything.

We work each other, my cock sliding nearly all the way out and then back in. The sound of our skin meeting is intoxicating, pushing me higher. She pants and cries out when I thrust harder, getting deeper, wanting every single inch to be encased by her. Everything fades away, and all I see is her.

I want to burn fast and hot.

She seems to have the same urgency, as if this moment might be our last.

I flip her on her back and slide back inside, the brief absence enough to make her gasp at the renewed contact. I take control, moving in and out of her, hard and fast. I hitch her leg up over my shoulder. *More.*

My free hand finds her pussy and plays with her clit, strumming her to the rhythm of my thrusts. "You're mine," I mutter hoarsely.

I bite her palm and grunt as I take her, the motion frenzied, more intense as she arches closer, her legs squeezing me in a vise.

"Always. Always. Always," I say, my voice like gravel.

I push into her faster, feeling the tingle at the base of my spine. We fuck like animals, and I'm about to blow. Sweat drips down my face and lands on her breasts. "Come for me," I push out, twisting on her nipple with my fingers.

Her eyes are wild as she comes apart again, her muscles milking my cock and sending me over into bliss with her.

With my heart still flying, I sag down next to her, my emotions all over the place. That was . . . fucking amazing.

She turns until we're lying face to face, our legs intertwined. A worried expression flits across her face.

"What's wrong?" I say, running my hand down her cheek.

She bites her lip. "Is it always like this with you? So . . . intense?"

Satisfaction fills me and I grin. "Best you ever had, huh?"

She rolls her eyes and pops me on the arm, making me grunt. It doesn't hurt, of course, but I like making her smile.

"Maybe," she admits as she props her head up with her elbow. "What about you? Was it the best?"

I grow serious as I stare into her eyes. "Everything is different with you. I've never had sex with someone I cared about, so yeah, it's mind blowing. Hell, usually by now I'm dressed and out the door." My heart squeezes. "I'm not leaving . . . unless you want me to."

TWENTY-FOUR

Rose

THE NEXT MORNING, I WAKE up before Spider. Sometime in the night, we left the fort, blew out the candles, and moved to the bed.

We slept curled up next to each other, spooning with my back to his chest. During the early hours, I felt his lips brush my shoulders, almost reverently . . . hopeful.

But this morning, as I look at the glare of the sun coming in through the blinds, guilt is brewing, especially as I check my phone.

I skim through texts.

All of them are from Trenton.

You okay? Sent at around the time the lights must have gone out. His apartment is about five blocks from here, but I imagine all the sirens and news reports probably alerted him of the blackout.

Another one was sent a few minutes later, probably around the time Spider knocked on my door.

Rose, I know you're up. You there? You scared?

Then, half an hour later, **Okay, you must be asleep. Good night. I love you.**

"Everything okay?" Spider murmurs, rising up to peek over my shoulder. His hair is everywhere, a small smile on his full lips.

I set my phone back down and try to push thoughts of Trenton away. I gaze over at Spider as he rubs his eyes and stretches. He looks . . . hot. I catch a glimpse of his broad chest from the covers and all I want to do is throw myself on top of him.

But I can't.

"Everything's great," I say brightly. But that isn't true. I'm worried about Trenton and what I've done.

I slide off the bed, wrapping the duvet around my naked body as I dart for the bathroom.

"Hey, come back here, woman. I'm not done with you." His voice is teasing, and it makes me smile a little.

I head to my dresser, feeling deliciously sore. "I have a class in a couple of hours. I need to shower and get out of here."

I'm not looking at him, but I know he's watching me. I hear him rustling around as he sits up in the bed.

"Rose?"

"Yeah?" I shuffle through my underwear drawer, my nervous fingers snatching at whatever I can find. I go with the white satin— plain, simple . . . meant for girls who don't cheat on their boyfriends.

"You okay?"

I look over at him as he stands up in his full naked glory, the sun creating a halo effect around his head.

I blink at the magnificence of him. Besides the incredible ink he has, his chest is tan and rippling with muscle. And the deliciously chiseled V that leads down to his waist is damn near the most beautiful piece of flesh I've ever seen. It directs my gaze straight to his cock, which is currently long and thick. My mouth wants to suck on it.

My body hums, needing him again.

He is without a doubt the most beautiful creature I've ever had.

And I *had* him for sure.

I want it again. Right now.

A wave of remorse hits.

I'm terrible! I'm supposed to meet Trenton for dinner tonight. How will I be able to face him?

Spider stalks over to me, and leans his palm on the wall behind me, unease on his face. "Are you having regrets?"

This man made me fall in love with him and then walked away.

"I'm not sure I can trust you, Spider. You left me."

He stares down at the rose on his hand. "I left you to let you breathe."

Emotion clogs my throat and I step away from him, sliding out of his reach.

He brings me back by grabbing my hand and lacing our fingers together, his expression moving from unease to determination. "What's wrong?"

I bite my lip. "I'm kinda in a hurry . . . I have a test I really should study for."

He runs his hand down my neck. "Don't make me beg to spend more time with you."

"Spider—"

He cuts me off and kisses me, his tongue tangling with mine as his hand slips under the duvet and cups my ass, pulling me against him. "This . . . this is what I want. Tell me you want me too."

"I do," I moan.

Every coherent thought I have flies out the window.

He knows he has me.

TWENTY-FIVE

Spider

WITH MY BLUE-MIRRORED AVIATORS AND a Yankees baseball cap pulled low over my eyes, I feel fairly incognito as I saunter out of the building and make my way down the street to the bakery to get Rose and I breakfast. I stop at the corner and see a shabbily dressed older man sitting on an old milk crate and playing a ukulele. He has a hungry look about him with gaunt features and a scraggly bit of gray scruff. His eyes are red and bleary.

That might have been me someday.

The small mutt that lounges beside the music man barks at me, as if reading my thoughts, making me smirk. I stop in front of him, getting jostled around, yet determined to stay and listen as the old man plays a little tune that sounds familiar, though I can't place it. I drop a hundred down in his open case.

He looks up at me. "May you find joy and happiness today."

I nod, turning to reply to him as I walk away. "Already have, and she's gorgeous."

I jog down to the bakery and stock up on a few things I think she might like—two croissant sandwiches with egg and bacon, several blueberry scones, and two strawberry muffins. On impulse, I grab some freshly baked chocolate chip cookies. We worked up a bit of an appetite last night, and I, for one, am starving.

"Hey, don't I know you?" the barista asks me as I pay in cash.

"Nope."

She narrows her eyes, studying me as she wraps up the cookies and adds them to the bulging bag of goodies. She eyes the tattoo on my neck. "You look like that guy Spider from Vital Rejects."

"Who?" I ask, plastering a bemused expression on my face.

She cocks her head. "Yeah, you're like his doppelganger."

Just give me my change, I think.

She leans in conspiratorially. "You can tell me. I won't tell anyone."

I exhale. "Yes, I'm Spider." After all, it's pretty obvious with the tattoo.

"OH MY GOD," she squeals.

I hold my hands up, motioning for her to quiet down. People are staring.

She licks her lips and flicks a strand of hair over her shoulder. "Hey, you know, you're my free pass."

My brow furrows. "Is that some kind of free coffee thing?"

She giggles. "No, it means I get to fuck you and my boyfriend has to be okay with it."

I blink, staring at her now instead of salivating over the bakery case.

She's a statuesque blonde with pretty features and a set of boobs that are tight.

"I don't fuck random people," I say. *Not anymore.*

She arches a brow. "Not according to all those supermarket rags." She grabs a notepad, scribbles something on it, and tosses it in the bag—her phone number, no doubt.

I fume, my mouth tightening. I fish it out and hand it back to her. "I don't want this."

A sullen look crosses her face. "Fine, I just thought you'd be into it is all."

I might have been two years ago—but not now.

A few minutes later, I'm back inside Rose's place with the bag and she's looking at me uncertainly. I figure she's thinking about Trenton, and what comes next. I'm terrified frankly. I want her to tell me she'll never see him again, but there's a distance in her eyes that gives me pause.

I run my eyes over her casual gray yoga pants and NYU sweatshirt. She takes my breath. "You look gorgeous."

"Thanks." She smiles hesitantly as I help myself to her cabinets and get us plates for the pastries.

We eat together, both of us quiet. I'm nervous; she's nervous. A few moments tick by as the room fills with silence. I watch her eat the muffin, my eyes on her perfect lips, the way her hair curls over her shoulder. My cock is hard, and all I can think about is spreading her out on the table. I tell myself to chill out. I don't want to overwhelm her.

She peeks up at me as she chews. "We had sex, and now things are weird."

I stuff the last bite of a croissant in my mouth. "I know how to make it not weird."

"Oh?" She arches a brow.

"Let's do it again," I say with a little growl.

She tucks a strand of hair behind her ear and lets out a shaky breath.

"What are you thinking?" I ask, leaning over the table to wipe a crumb from her cheek.

She doesn't speak, but her eyes are low, her lashes fluttering.

"Tell me what you're thinking." My voice is verging on pleading.

"I want you so much, I can't breathe. I can't think straight—"

She doesn't get to finish her sentence.

I sweep her up in my arms and carry her back to the bedroom.

TWENTY-SIX

Rose

'M A HORRIBLE PERSON.

A cheater.

A liar.

I sit on the subway, my gut churning as I rub my forehead.

All I think about is my time with Spider.

About how we had sexy times all over my apartment today.

He is intoxicating.

Fascinating.

Enthralling.

Mesmerizing.

He is all I can think about.

It's happening all over again, and I'm scared he's going to ruin me.

The subway clangs to halt and I look up to realize it's my stop. *Trenton . . . God.* My gut twists as I think about how to tell him.

I enter his company's suite inside the huge office building and stop at the front desk that sits in the center of the room. The lobby has two windows, each decorated with custom upholstery. Along the wall sits a line of cushy, formal-looking chairs in a Queen Anne style, reeking of old money and family tradition. It reminds me of Highland Park.

The receptionist is turned around filing papers, so I clear my throat to get her attention. She turns around to face me and I do a double take.

"Aria?" My voice is surprised, and I'm fairly certain my mouth might be open.

The last I heard from Trenton, she was still in Texas and attending college. Yes, she's his cousin, but he's rarely seen her except for holidays when they were at the same family gatherings. I avoided any event where I knew she would be, but I did see her once at a wedding for another cousin. We barely spoke to each other, which was easy enough to do since it was crowded.

Why didn't he tell me she moved here?

She's still beautiful, of course, her brown hair shorter and cut in a blunt, straight style. Wearing a short red pencil skirt and a printed button-up shirt, she looks amazing. I glance down at my yoga pants and sweatshirt. I'm practically a hobo compared to her.

"Helloooo, Rose!" she says, dragging out the greeting in her soft southern drawl. "I started last week. Didn't Trenton tell you?" She arches her brow.

I shake my head.

Her laugh tinkles across the darkly paneled office, grating on my nerves. "Well, here I am . . . the new office clerk." She holds her arms out and does a full pirouette in her black stilettos.

I nod. "Trenton's been so busy with that new case, I guess he forgot to tell me."

She smiles tightly, not showing me her teeth, her eyes raking over my attire and landing squarely on my red Converse. "You've got something on your sweatshirt there," she says, pointing at me and squinting with a look on her face like she smells something bad.

I look down and see a tiny spot of white, which I figure is either sugar from the muffin Spider brought me this morning or, more embarrassingly, my toothpaste.

It feels like Highland Park all over again, and I'm right back in my greasy Jo's Diner polo.

The tension that has always been between us rears its head, and I exhale.

I return her tight smile. "So, Trenton's dad got you this job? Couldn't find anything else in the city?"

"We're family and we do stick together." She sighs, placing her hand on her heart, flashing a huge diamond engagement ring. "I'm just lucky to have my real family, ya know? So many people don't these days."

My teeth grind at the insinuation.

She leans in over the counter. "Of course, I hope we can work past our differences. Trenton is my cousin, and I want us to be friends."

"I didn't think I had the right pedigree to be your friend."

She shrugs. "We just moved here, and I'm positive Trenton will want to hang out with us. This is a rather large city, and we *are* family."

"We?" My eyes land on her diamond again, nearly blinded by its size.

She smiles broadly and holds out her hand. "Garrett, of course. It's going to be a summer wedding after he finishes his first year of medical school here."

My hands fist, but I play it cool, smiling. "Splendid. Now, I'm going to see Trenton."

She calls out after me as I march down to his small office, but I ignore her, opening the door wide.

He stands behind his desk, his sandy blond hair rumpled as if he's run his hands through it several times. Sitting on a chair next to his desk is his assistant Vivien, a stylish lady in her fifties who I met the first week he started. Papers and folders litter the room.

"Rose!" His face is lined with a frown as he spots me then Aria right behind me.

"I told her you were busy, but she ignored me," Aria says.

He waves at her over my shoulder. "It's fine. I can say hi to my girl."

"Hey," I say, coming into the room and getting a little thrill from shutting the door in Aria's face.

He comes around the oak desk and meets me halfway, giving me a hug. "Now there's a sight for sore eyes." He kisses me soundly on the lips, and I reflexively kiss him back, feeling wrong—horribly, horribly wrong.

Vivien says hello, her gaze immediately back on her work.

"So, Aria? That's new."

He smirks. "Yeah, sorry I forgot to tell you. I hope we can work things out with them . . . if you're comfortable with Garrett."

Comfortable? He's a douchebag. I frown. "I'm not."

He caresses his hand down my arm. "They're engaged, so he's going to be part of my family. Maybe we should cut him some slack."

I start to say something but clamp my mouth shut when I realize that at this point, Garrett is a moot point.

There's a reason I'm here, and it doesn't have jack to do with

Aria or Garrett.

"Look, I'm sorry I didn't call first, I just . . . needed to talk to you. Maybe you can take a break and we can hit the coffee shop across the street?"

He checks his watch, a look of regret on his face. "Can it wait? This client is coming in tomorrow for a conference, and we just got some last-minute additions to the investment portfolio so we aren't prepared." He kisses me on the forehead. "I promise you, once the next few days are over, I'll be all over you, but you have to let me get this done."

I fiddle with my backpack, not meeting his eyes. "We *need* to talk."

He tilts my chin up, blue eyes studying me, a frown knitting his brow. "Is anyone dying? Is everyone okay in Dallas?"

"This is about *us*, Trenton."

Impatience flits across his chiseled features. "I'm at work, Rose. This job is new, and Vivien and I have a deadline."

Vivien clears her throat, and he takes a step back in her direction. "I'll text you later. Dinner maybe?"

I nod. "I'll pop by your place and we can order in."

He nods at me absently, already striding back to his desk.

I send them a final look, although neither of them notices. Hitching my backpack up on my shoulder, I head through his door and out into the main office.

TWENTY-SEVEN

Spider

WHERE ARE YOU?

I hit send on the text to Rose as I sit inside a small, dimly lit bar-slash-bookstore next to our apartment building. I try to not let panic eat at me, but when she told me back at her place that she was going to talk to Trenton after class, worry took up all the space in my head.

She said she was going to break up with him, but there was doubt on her face. Was the doubt about Trenton or me?

Fuck. I don't know. I'm worried. I just want her back and in my arms. That's all.

She is a fucking flower, and I want to open every single petal, one by one.

Sebastian sits across from me and sips on a beer. Both of us are wearing ball caps and aviators and keeping our chins down. Maybe the sunglasses are too much at night, but there's weirder shit in this town. Sebastian has already had a group of reporters somehow get a picture of him on his balcony at the Madison Hotel. Rocco and Max are hanging out at a friend's place until the concert.

Mila, our PR girl, walks over from where she was looking for some kind of romance book.

I recall how I asked her to come over that day Rose showed up at my apartment in Dallas. I knew Mila had a soft spot for me and I exploited it, asking her to pretend we'd had sex and to turn her skirt backward. Of course, she agreed, and, well . . . the rest is history.

We messed around a little in LA, but it was half-hearted, and we never fucked. Once she realized I was using her to push Rose out of my head, she moved on, and she's currently dating some country music star.

Dressed in her usual—a pink miniskirt and a white shirt—she slaps down a book of poems about love on the table. "If she loves *Jane Eyre* and you want to woo her, you better up your game. Maybe read her some poetry." She chuckles, her eyes taking in the people around us, making sure no one is eavesdropping. She's our little bulldog and goes the extra mile to protect us.

"I know how to woo." I waggle my brows.

Yes, they know that I gave her the book, but I didn't tell them about our night together. I didn't even tell them she's my neighbor. I don't know why I can't own up to the happiness I'm feeling. Maybe it's because I'm afraid if I talk too much about it, she'll disappear. Like Cate and Mum. The thought of losing her again . . . crushes me.

Mila gags. "Please don't tell me about your sex life. I might vomit."

I smirk.

Mila stares at me, as if she's trying to figure me out. "You love her," she says, a satisfied gloat on her face. "The mighty Spider has fallen."

I blink. "I don't know what you mean."

"Just can't say the *L* word can you?" Sebastian smirks as he tips back his beer.

I take a sip of my sparkling water. "We're not all as in touch with our feelings as you are." But, he is right. I don't use the word *love*.

"Pity."

"Sod off, wanker."

"You sod off," he says.

I laugh. "You don't even know what *sod off* means."

"It doesn't mean grass?" he asks with a twinkle in his eye.

"No, arsehole."

Mila takes the seat next to me. "I love all your bad words, but *wanker* is my favorite," she says.

I chuckle and she gives me a fist bump.

She wraps an arm around me and gives me a side hug. "I'm happy you saw her. Have you decided what's next? Are you going to invite her to your art opening?" She smiles.

I hug her back and kiss her on the cheek. "Yeah."

I don't see Rose come into the bar and watch us.

I don't see her when she leaves.

TWENTY-EIGHT

Rose

'M ALMOST BACK TO THE apartment when my gaze goes to the lights from the bar and bookstore across the street. A favorite hangout, I usually stop by after classes to check out their books and baked goods. Not your typical bookstore, it's dark and cozy and serves awesome baked pretzels.

I decide to pop in and grab a pretzel . . . or two. Maybe Spider is home and I will share with him. I know his concert is tomorrow night, so it's possible he's practicing late, but you never know. My phone is dead or I'd text and ask him.

I go inside and make it to the bar as a familiar laugh catches my attention. Taking my pretzel to-go from the cashier, I turn, my eyes landing squarely on Spider's back and shoulders. A ball cap mostly hides his hair, but I know that laugh. A pretty brunette in a super short skirt is leaned over in his space. Another guy sits a bit away from them, also in a ball cap.

The girl . . .

I know her.

My stomach drops and nausea swirls as I watch her hug Spider. He puts his hands on her shoulders and kisses her cheek.

My breath stops—hell, the whole world stops.

There's something between them, an easiness that speaks to many years together.

I lick my lips, feeling lightheaded, my heart open and bleeding.

I play back the memory I have of her . . . she comes out of his building with her skirt on backward . . . he tells me he just fucked her.

"Hey, you okay?" asks the cashier who handed over my pretzel.

I swallow and nod, tears pricking at my eyes, words sticking in my throat as I lean back against the wall. In a blur of motion, I dash out the door and into the night.

I COME HOME IN A daze. By nine, my phone is charging and has pinged with texts from Trenton asking if I'm coming over and several from Spider wanting to know where I am.

I ignore them all.

Anne tries to call me and I hit decline.

A few minutes later she sends me a text that they are coming to New York in a few days.

I don't care. I just want to wallow and forget what I saw tonight.

I force the pretzel down and drink a glass of wine . . . and then another. Pretty soon I have the bottle sitting on the coffee table so I can drink straight from it.

By the time Oscar arrives home around ten, I'm piled up on

the couch with a fur blanket over me, propped up on pillows, crying over a movie on Lifetime.

He sits down and puts his arm around me. I called him earlier on his break and told him everything. "I'm here, baby girl. It's time for an Oscar Intervention."

I wave at him to be quiet, although I really don't want him to. I need someone to talk to, but I'm scared to face the truth: Spider was hanging out with the girl from Dallas. Who is she to him? Why did he kiss her? Why did they look like they've been *together* for a long time? He always told me he didn't do long term with girls . . . but obviously she's different.

Oscar considers me. "I think you need to stop hiding over here and get your big girl panties on."

I sniff. "Can it wait? The hero's about to find out that the girl had his secret baby ten years ago."

"You're watching shit TV to avoid your problems. I believe in your psychology classes they call it *classic avoidance*."

I grab a tissue and huff. "You've been reading my textbooks again."

He shrugs. "He's right next door. You need to march over to that apartment and ask him what's going on."

"But shouldn't I finish *My Secret Billionaire Baby Daddy*?"

He snatches the remote from the coffee table, clicks off the TV, and gives me a serious look.

"Now I'll never know what happens!"

Oscar is having none of it. "Maybe what you saw isn't the way it really is."

"She was hugging all over him," I say. "And he was looking at her like he cared about her." My voice cracks.

God. I have to know. I need to get to the bottom of this.

With a deep exhale, I stand, straightening my yoga pants and wrinkled shirt. I'm not wearing much makeup and my hair is up in a loose topknot that has long since decided to slide off to the side.

I head to the door.

"Wait!" Oscar screeches. "You can't go over there like that. At least put on some shoes and brush out your hair."

"Why?"

"Because you smell like stale wine and look like a homeless person." He flicks his eyes at the bottle of chardonnay in my hand. "At *least* leave the wine here."

I take a swig. "I don't want to lose my buzz."

He fusses around me, tightening my hair and wiping at my eyes. "Just let me blot this mascara."

I put on my Converse and stumble out the door, stabilizing myself against the hallway walls. I'm a bit drunk and I don't care.

I knock on his door and it flies open.

It's her.

At ten o'clock at night.

In his apartment.

If that isn't more clear than before, then I don't know what is.

She opens the door about two feet then slowly eases it shut as she eyes me warily.

I snort. Clearly she is leery of me.

Her eyes sweep over me, widening on the bottle clutched in my hand. "You delivering the Chinese food?"

"Do I look like I have Chinese food?" I slur, the word *food* coming out as *lood.*

Her brow furrows, but it doesn't take away from her prettiness. "Do I know you?"

I flip her off. She should know me from Dallas, but it's likely

I look different with my copper hair up in a knot and my frumpy hanging out clothes. Also, she probably didn't pay as much attention to me as I did her.

She cranes her neck out into the hall and checks it out carefully. "How did you get up to this floor?"

I ignore that and wipe at my mouth, squinting in dismay at the bit of crumbs that come off on my hand. Oscar was right—I look like a hobo.

But I don't give a shit, my head screams.

I point my finger at her, using the hand holding the bottle. "I want to see Spider. Now."

She scrunches her forehead up as if she's confused and scoots farther over to block my vision into the apartment. "I don't know who that is."

"Liar. I know he's staying here."

She narrows her eyes at me. "I suggest you leave before I call the police."

I laugh. "The last thing he wants is a police report about a chick fight inside his building."

She cocks her head. "You look very familiar—"

I don't let her finish, instead shoving the door. She pushes back and we tussle back and forth.

I briefly think I'll probably regret this in the morning, but right now, I don't care.

I have alcohol and Converse on my side while she is tiny with a pair of pink clogs that look like they belong on a ten-year-old. I shove her aside and march into the foyer of the apartment while she tugs on my arm. I shake her off. It's easy, especially because I'm running on adrenaline and pure rage.

A quick glance around his apartment shows an empty den and

kitchen. Clothes are everywhere, some hanging in dry-cleaning bags. Music sheets litter the floor along with blank art canvases. I pause on them briefly, wondering about them, but get hung up on a soft pink cardigan draped over the chair in the living room. I cringe, knowing it's hers.

I twirl around. "Where is he?"

She sends me a livid look as she pulls out her phone. "You're trespassing, and I'm calling the doorman. I'll let him deal with you."

I knock the phone out of her hand. She really isn't a match for me, not with the self-defense classes I still take and the anger burning in my gut.

"Where is he?" I push the words out. "Just tell me."

She sucks in a shuddering breath and for a moment I see fear flitting across her face, but then she seems to rally, her resolve strengthening as she circles around me, blocking me from moving farther into the apartment.

My eyes go to the bedroom, and my heart drops.

She stiffens her shoulders. "He's in the shower. Happy?"

My eyes bounce back to the bedroom, and the deafening silence allows me to hear the water running. A beat later, it clicks off.

"You need to go now," she says, shooing at me with her hands as if I'm an errant fly she wants out of the apartment.

Spider's voice yells from the bedroom. "Hey, I left my stuff in the laundry. Be a love and bring me some boxers, will you? Please?" He chuckles, the sound drifting into where we are.

I feel odd as if I'm not really in the room, but in a movie watching as the girl realizes the hero really *is* a douchebag. I can't avoid the truth anymore.

I still love him so much.

I don't know how it's possible, but this time it hurts more. It hammers at my heart a little harder, a little deeper. I rub at my chest, feeling sick. Like I might throw up.

We made love.

He said I was his.

No—that was just fucking to him.

Leopards don't change their spots. *Past behavior is the best predictor for future behavior.*

Loving him is hopeless, and if there's one thing I know is true, it's that I don't deserve this kind of love.

Pink Cardigan glares at me. She's been on her phone talking to someone. "I called the doorman downstairs. He's on his way up."

Without another word, I stumble out of the door she's widened for me then she slams it behind me.

Wearily, I walk the few feet back to my own place, my bravado gone, my spirit broken. I open the door and go inside.

TWENTY-NINE

Spider

THE NEXT DAY AROUND ELEVEN, I knock on Rose's door, but no one answers. The concert is tonight and I have a ton of things to do, but I'm itching to see her face. I'm wondering if she can come watch us run through our set. I want to tell her about my upcoming art show and maybe introduce her to the rest of the band.

I'm worried as I stand there and knock.

Last night, I'd knocked on her door after Mila dropped off my dry cleaning, but Oscar answered and said Rose was sick and didn't want to see me. I wanted to push my way inside and check on her, especially since she hadn't replied to any of my earlier texts, but Oscar's tight face made me pause. Something felt off but I couldn't put my finger on it. It made me worry about Trenton and what happened between them. I decided to give her some space, so I eased off and went back to my place.

It wasn't until this morning in the shower when I was playing back the evening, especially the part about the random girl who showed up drunk at my flat, that everything clicked. Mila mentioned the girl looked familiar but she couldn't place her. She assumed she was one of the hardcore groupies who follow us from city to city, trying to find ways into our hotel rooms and homes. One time in LA, a girl even hid in my car and slept there, surprising the shit out of me when I crawled inside to head to the studio the next day.

But . . .

What if this random girl had been Rose?

I mean, I didn't tell Mila that she lived next door, and if Mila had opened the door to Rose before I had a chance to explain to her about Dallas . . .

With a knot in my stomach, I knock on her door again, this time harder. I get nothing but silence.

Pulling out my phone, I type a quick text to her. **Are you home? Are you feeling better?**

Agitated, I lean against the hallway and wait for her reply but get nothing. I rake a hand through my hair and pace up and down the hall, wondering what to do next. The girl showing up at my door is really bothering me . . . it feels ominous, and I want to shake it off.

I have to know if it was Rose.

I send another text. **Did you come to my apartment last night?**

Yes, is the immediate reply. **I saw her.**

Fuck.

Dread pools in my gut as I picture the scene the way Rose might have perceived it. It's not good.

It's not what you think, I tell her. **I can explain but not**

through text. Open your door.

> **I'm at the library. I'm turning my phone off. Goodbye.**

I slap my hand on the wall and push off, feeling frustrated. I don't know what's going on with her. Is she angry? Is she going to let me explain? *Fuck!*

Maybe I should go to the library and find her. I'm assuming it's the NYU library, but I don't know for sure. It could be any library. Antsy and jittery, I decide it's not helping to stand around, so I shake it off and leave to run my errands.

My first stop is at the art gallery in Soho where my show will be in a few days. It's an invitation only event where several musicians will be showing their work. I've been working on it for months, and I'm looking forward to seeing it come to fruition.

I waltz in and Jenny, the gallery owner, meets me with a wide grin. A blonde with a broad genuine smile, she shakes my hand enthusiastically. "You want a sneak peek of everything?"

I shake my head. "Just here to pick up more invites for the show. I didn't think my father and his wife were going to make it, but they are. I also need one for a girl."

Or at least I hope I do.

Father called yesterday to tell me they were coming to see my show. He hadn't known for sure because Anne broke her leg on a skiing trip a few weeks ago and he didn't know if she'd be ready to travel. Thankfully, she is, and I'm glad. It feels like Anne tolerates me most of the time, and truth be told, I'm fine with that.

It's my dad I want to secure a solid relationship with.

I told him about seeing Rose and he wished me well.

I take the cardstock invitations from Jenny and leave. With unease still eating at me about Rose, I get in my car to head to the venue for the show. I type out one more text to her. **Can I see you**

tonight after the concert?

I get no reply.

THIRTY

Rose

FTER READING SPIDER'S TEXT, I put my phone away. I told him I was going to turn it off, but I'm not. I just can't talk to him right now.

I close my eyes and lean my head back against the wall in the library where I'm currently hiding out, supposedly working on a research paper for one of my classes.

I pull out the cherry-flavored Gatorade Oscar tucked in my backpack this morning and chug it down along with a few Saltines—lunch of champions.

After forcing myself to take a few more notes on my laptop, I wrap things up and head to my weekend Krav Maga class at a small gym on Brewster Street. As soon as I moved to New York, I signed up for the course I'd started in Dallas. Employing efficient movements and gut instincts, my instructor is one of the best in the city.

After a grueling lesson where my partner slams me down on

the mat more times than I think is necessary—though my body somehow likes it—I shower there and change into my usual black slacks and button-up white blouse with the lace collar, my uniform for Bono's. I blow out my hair and pull it up in a topknot. My only makeup is my deep red lipstick and some mascara.

Tonight, I'm working the dinner shift. It's the weekend, so things will be hopping, and I'm glad because I won't have time to think about Spider.

As I walk in the door, I receive another text from Anne. She sent one last night saying they were coming to New York and I never replied. I reply back and ask about their plans, anxious to know if I'll see Bella. She tells me they're coming without Bella and staying at their penthouse since the painters have finished. She invites me to dinner Sunday night, and I tell her yes since I'm not working.

It's her next text that throws me.

We'll be attending Spider's art show on Monday. Are you going?

Art show? I know nothing about it.

I'm not sure how to answer her.

One of the managers calls my name and I know it's time to get to work. Wanting to know more about the show but also needing to not get fired, I tuck my phone away.

At nine, when the dinner rush has slowed, I'm serving a table of four their entrees when I hear a familiar voice behind me.

"I guess you've come a long way when you go from Jo's Diner to Manhattan. Yet, you're still a waitress. How . . . quaint."

My teeth grit as I turn to see Aria, Trenton, and Garrett being seated by the hostess, who sends me an apologetic glance after Aria's comment. "These guys want your section."

I sigh. "Great."

Trenton gives me a sweeping hug. "We're here to celebrate. I got everything turned in on time and the client is referring me to some of his buddies."

I blink, suddenly remembering that I was supposed to pop over to his place last night to talk.

He doesn't mention that I never replied to his texts, probably because Aria and Garrett are here.

"That's awesome. Congratulations." My voice is flat.

Aria narrows her eyes at me. "And of course you recall Garrett, my *fiancé*." She emphasizes the last word.

I focus my gaze on him. *Screw you,* my eyes say.

Garrett has lost hair on top and looks sour and a bit sullen, his shoulders stiff as he watches me. A slight sneer curls his lips before disappearing in the blink of an eye, a micro-expression, those things people do when they want to hide how they really feel. Most of them are completely involuntary. It's like when you walk into someone's house and you smell cat pee—you can't hide the brief expression of displeasure.

I exhale and look at Trenton.

Today . . . with all three of them here, my head just . . . hurts.

"I'm not going to be your waitress," I state.

"That's just pure laziness," Aria murmurs. "Don't you make money on tips?"

"I don't want your money." I face Trenton, a ball of anger building. "You brought them here . . . without even asking me?"

His face scrunches up as if dislikes my tone. "They're family. If this is about me working—"

"No." I hold my hand up. "This is about you and me."

He must read something on my face because he takes my elbow and leads me away from Aria and Garrett until we're standing a few feet away near the front door.

"What's wrong with you, Rose?" His voice borders between irritated and surprised.

Normally, I'm easy and ready to go along with whatever he wants.

The air is tense, and I know this moment is about truth, about being true to myself when I haven't been for a long time. I look Trenton over, my gut realizing that I've just been passing time with him, content with our relationship but not really happy. He doesn't get who I am and what I need.

"I can't see you anymore."

Shock settles on his face. "I-I . . . I can't believe this. What did I do wrong?"

"Nothing. It's not you. It's just . . . we've been drifting apart for a while."

He sighs. "We'd see each other more if you'd move in with me and stop working—"

"I'm not *it* for you," I say, cutting him off.

His eyes sharpen. "What's this really about?"

My lips tighten.

He watches me. "Is this about Spider? I might have been drunk the night I saw you two together, but I'd have to be an idiot to not see that he wants you."

In for a penny, in for a pound.

I clench my fists for strength. "I had sex with Spider . . . this week." I rip the Band-Aid off, ready to get to the healing part.

His face goes white and a muscle flexes in his jaw. His chest expands as he inhales a deep breath.

I nod. "I'm sorry to hurt you. I really am. We haven't been right . . . for a long time."

He's angry now, his neck and face turning red. It's the most reaction I've seen out of him in a long time. "Everyone knows he's on drugs, Rose. He'll never be true to you."

His last words kill me, because they might be true. I can't think about that right now, and I focus on telling the truth. "I love him more than anything." More than you.

Emotion ripples across his face and he shakes his head at me. His hands clench, and I can tell he's wrestling with his feelings, deciding on what to say to me. I prepare myself for him to lash out. He doesn't disappoint and the words he uses only prove that he and I were never meant to be together. "I should have listened to my friends. You really are just trash, Rose."

Then he turns and stalks back to where Aria and Garrett await. I watch as he briefly tells them something and they turn to look at me. Without another word, they gather their things from the table where the hostess placed them and walk out the door.

AFTER MY SHIFT, I'M EXHAUSTED. It's almost midnight and all I want to do is fall in the bed.

As I walk home, Oscar texts that he's staying overnight with Axe again but will be home in the morning to make us Sunday breakfast. I tap out a quick reply telling him to invite Axe over too. I'm happy that at least one of us has a great love life.

When I arrive at my building, the doorman lets me up, and I enter the elevator and lean against the wall.

"Hold the door," Spider calls out just before it closes.

I hold the door as a reflex and he enters. I try to ignore his male scent and the way his shirt clings to his broad chest. His hair is damp as if he's showered recently, and I figure his concert is over and he's cleaned up. He stands next to me, and I should move away, but I'm weak and want to be close to him for a little longer.

"I could barely focus at the concert. Are you okay?" His eyes search mine, moving down to take in my server outfit.

I ignore his question.

"I was at work . . . and I broke up with Trenton."

Relief crosses his face. "Thank fuck." He pushes a strand of hair behind my ear. "Were you ever sick last night or was that all about Mila? I want to explain that—"

I stiffen, my jaw clenching as I interrupt him. "She's the girl that was at your place the day you left Dallas?"

He gives me a short nod. "Look, she's just our PR person and I've known her for years. It's not—"

I cut him off, my words sharp. "I saw you with her at the bar across the street. Then, I knocked on your door and she answered . . . *while you were taking a shower.*"

He lets out a breath. "Rose, listen to me. I never slept with her. I only pretended that day in Dallas. I called her to come over and put on a show to make sure you didn't ruin your life and maybe follow me to LA. I hated doing it and I hated walking away from you that day, but I had to." He pauses, his face anxious as he studies my face, looking for my reaction. "I would have told you sooner but . . . it's been crazy and we haven't had time."

There's a ring of truth in his voice.

But . . .

"You two seem very chummy. Did you have a relationship with her at any point in LA?"

"We never had sex." His eyes are pleading with me to understand, and part of me does. He used her to get to me, to hammer it home.

"She's a friend and a co-worker, Rose. And last night, she was dropping off my dry cleaning. That's it. I don't feel that way about her. I never have. It's you. Just you."

I soften at his words but tears prick at my eyes as I think back to that day in Dallas. "I know you thought I was too young and that you were too screwed up, but I would have gone to the ends of the world with you."

He looks tortured. "I wasn't ready."

"Are you ready now?"

He nods. "Yes."

But there's an uncertain look on his face, as if he's unsure . . . and it scares me. I can't figure out where his head is.

I need more from him.

I need the *words.* "Do you love me?"

There's a struggle on his face, and he just stares at me.

Clarity arrives as I take him in. With Spider it's always been about people he lost, but it's time for him to figure out that I'm not leaving him.

I chew on my bottom lip and lay it all out on the line. "You say that I'm yours, but all I see is a guy who wants me on his terms. You show up and just expect me to fall back in your arms when you should have told me about Mila the first time you saw me. You could have told me the night of the storm. You should have found me *today* somehow and explained it to me—and you didn't. Your hesitation and lack of commitment terrify me. You're afraid of how big this thing is between us." I pause. "I need more, Spider. I want fucking epic. I want someone to love me with the same intensity I feel for *him.*" I suck in a breath. "And until you give it to me, I can't see you."

He exhales as he stares at me, emotion burning in his eyes.

The elevator door opens and we step out. He watches me as I fumble around in my purse for keys. Finally I find them and unlock my door.

I turn to look at him, my heart hurting.

He's still standing there when I shut the door.

I rest against it and let the tears I've held at bay all day finally come.

THIRTY-ONE

Rose

THE FOLLOWING DAY, OSCAR AND I show up at Robert and Anne's penthouse for dinner. Oscar hasn't seen them much over the years, just a few times when they would pop in to New York for a quick visit.

"How do I look?" he asks me, seeming anxious as he straightens his purple Tom Ford tie as we stand in front of the heavy cream-colored double doors, about to knock.

"Awesome."

He clears his throat, an odd look on his face. He's nervous and I frown, reading his body language. "What is it? You're not telling me something."

He exhales, his shoulders dipping as he turns to face me. "There's something I need to tell you. Maybe I should have told you a long time ago—but I didn't."

"Okay, that sounds ominous. Are you really straight?"

He snorts and gestures to his pale gray suit with tightly creased skinny slacks and argyle yellow socks. "Does this ensemble say straight to you?"

"No."

"Right." He fluffs out his hair.

"Spill. You're keeping secrets from me. Are you and Axe getting married?"

He sighs. "I wish. No, Robert asked me not to tell you, but remember how I told you I got a last minute scholarship for NYU and that's how I was able to come to New York?"

I nod. "Yea, you always told me you got the underprivileged-smart-kid-who-also-happens-to-be-gay scholarship. I recall your letter was very last minute and I was worried for you."

Oscar grimaces. "My letter wasn't late. It came and the scholarship was denied. I just couldn't tell you because I knew how much you wanted NYU for both of us."

Oh. "Okay, so how did you get the money?"

Oscar gives me a look. "Robert . . . or Spider . . . I don't know which one for sure . . . footed the bill for everything."

My mouth flaps open and I quickly close it. I shake my head. "Stop joking. What's going on?"

He exhales. "Four years ago, one day after Spring Fling, I got this call from Spider. He said he just wanted to check in on you."

I'm in shock. "I can't believe you didn't tell me! You know how much I would have wanted to know that!"

"You were already with Trenton, and honestly, I just didn't want you to be sad or to go off and try to see him in LA." He gives me a look.

I nod, remembering how depressed I'd been. I might have gone to LA. I don't know.

"Anyway, he asked a few questions and wanted to know if I

was going to NYU with you, and I told him the whole story . . . that I'd been accepted but my scholarship didn't come through. That seemed to be the end of it."

"But it wasn't?"

He shakes his head. "A few days later, Robert showed up at my door with papers to sign from a foundation that paid for my entire education. All I had to do was contact the foundation each semester with my total and they'd pay it. The address of the foundation was a place in LA. That's why I think it was Spider who paid for it."

My heart is pounding and my head is trying to wrap around all this information. "Why wouldn't Robert want me to know?"

He shrugs. "I don't know. Maybe he didn't want you digging deeper and running to LA. He asked me to not tell you, and he was so nice about it, and I was just so thankful to have the opportunity to live our dream here in the city that I let it go. It was a lot of money, Rose."

The door opens, interrupting any more talk.

Robert and Anne greet us with hugs at the door, but I'm still reeling. I'm not sure I can stay. I'm not sure I can eat a thing . . . but I push through because part of me is holding out hope that Spider is coming. I just want to see him—even if we aren't together. That's all.

Anne gazes at my low-cut, hip-hugging red dress and takes a deep breath.

"I like tight dresses so don't even go there," I say with a smile, softening my words.

She nods and hooks her arm in mine and leads me into the dining room. I see there's another place setting across from me.

My heart dips.

"Is Spider coming?"

"He was invited, but sends his regrets," Robert says, his tone inquisitive, his eyes watchful as he looks at me.

It stings that he didn't come. "Ah." I clear my throat, needing to talk, needing to find out what the hell is going on. "Oscar told me you . . . or Spider . . . paid his tuition. Is there anything else you aren't telling me?"

He looks at Anne and they seem to have some kind of silent communication. She nods.

"Yes," he says. "Why don't you come into the study and we can talk before we eat."

I nod.

Finally. Some answers.

THIRTY-TWO

Spider

GOD, I WISH I STILL drank whiskey.

But then I guess I wouldn't be able to run five miles like I can now.

I kick up my pace, jogging through the trail in Central Park, but no matter how hard I try to keep my focus, keep my breathing tight and even, I feel unbalanced and off.

I don't have Rose.

Nothing is right.

My phone has been ringing off and on for twenty minutes, and I finally come to a stop on the stone bridge that overlooks the park then pull it out of my pocket to check.

It's Father.

"Hiya." I breathe heavily into the phone as I take a seat on a nearby bench. "Did you get your invitation to the show?"

"Spider . . ." His voice is quiet yet strong at the same time. "I have some bad news."

My head runs in a million directions. "Is it Rose?"

"No, no. We can't make your show tonight. Bella has come down with a high fever, and we want to get back to Dallas. Anne and I have a flight out in just a few hours. I just wanted you to know. I hate to miss it, son. I really mean that."

"Can I do anything?"

He laughs softly. "Not unless you want to hold a crying toddler for a few hours."

I laugh.

He sobers up, a long sigh coming from him.

"There's something else?" I ask.

I picture him nodding, his face stern. "Rose came over last night. I told her everything."

Now it's my turn to exhale. I pace back and forth across the small path, phone to my ear, thinking. "What did she say?"

"Not much."

"Ah." Disappointment rushes over me.

What did I expect?

"I'm sorry, son. I hope it works out for you both."

THIRTY-THREE

Rose

'M ALL NERVES WALKING INTO the gallery. Oscar is next to me, a somber, contemplative expression on his face, and I guess he's still mulling over the conversation we had last night with Robert.

I think back to the folder he gave me, the one with receipts for Oscar's and my tuition for NYU, the total cost over four hundred thousand dollars, all paid in increments as Spider rocketed to success over the past four years. Robert even told me that Spider negotiated that I'd get to attend NYU as part of his terms of leaving me. He also wanted to pay for it . . . just something he wanted to do for me.

It boggled my brain that Robert gave him half a million dollars to leave and then he turned right back around and gave most of it to me and Oscar.

Also enclosed in the folder was a beautifully written invitation with the address to the gallery in Soho.

I'm here tonight to ask him why.

Why . . . everything.

The first person I see is Mila.

Our eyes meet across the room and she starts, her face paling as she sets her drink down on a passing waiter's tray and pushes through the crowd to get to us.

I stiffen, my back tightening.

Oscar sends me side-eye. "Incoming bitch?"

"We'll see," I murmur.

"Dammit. I should have brought my brass knuckles." He links his arm with mine. "I got you, baby girl. Me and you, we might just be white trash from Texas, but we look good doing it."

"You look delightful, by the way," he says. "I'm glad you wore the white dress—makes you look like a bride. On the other hand, the approaching vision in pink is a bit hard to look at for too long."

"She reminds me of cotton candy, right?" I look at Oscar, my face grimacing. "Maybe this wasn't a good idea."

He shakes his head. "No, just listen to her. You came this far. We're here and there's free champagne and shrimp. A man has to eat."

The vision in the pink maxi dress with a million sequins stops in front of us. I have to squint so she doesn't hurt my eyes.

"So you're Rose," she says, eyeing me carefully, as if I were a rabid dog that might bite her. "I was so nervous in Dallas that I barely looked at you. You're also different from the pictures he drew of you . . . although tonight is the first time I'm seeing them."

What pictures?

Mila is still talking. "I'm a bit of a ditz. I had no clue who you were when you came to Spider's door. I thought you were some drunk groupie."

"Would that have made a difference in how you treated me?"

A horrified expression crosses her face. "Of course! It's . . . you're . . . his Rose."

Mila touches my arm, rather tentatively. "Look, I'm not into him anymore. If I were, they'd be no way we could work together." Her eyes are wide and direct as she looks at me. "I'm really sorry for thinking you were a crazy stalker fan."

People who lie tend to look up and to the left.

She isn't, and I believe her.

We stare at each other, me remembering her and Spider kissing all those years ago, and my pain must show in my eyes because she nudges me toward the entrance to the art room where guests are drifting in and out. "Look, just go in. I don't think you'll regret it. If you still have questions afterward, I'll answer them, but I don't think you will."

Oscar and I walk away and enter the room as a hostess hands us programs with information about the show. With a high vaulted ceiling, spacious skylights, and white walls, the art takes up all the attention.

Guests mill around everywhere, some I recognize.

"Holy Mary Tyler Moore, is that Sting over in the corner?" Oscar hisses in my ear.

I glance to where his eyes have darted, toward the end of the room. "Looks like him. You should go see. I'm going to start at the beginning and make my way across the room. I'll meet you there?"

He pats my hand. "You sure?"

I nod, wanting to be alone.

As I begin the show on Spider's side of the room, I see right away that the pieces are done in charcoal, like his sister's. I move from piece to piece, realizing it's organized as an autobiographical journey. There's one of Cate playing in the snow outside their childhood home. I study them intently, noting the bold strokes and modern feel. I smile. He really is so incredibly talented.

Is there anything he can't do?

I gasp when I come to one of me . . . waiting tables at Jo's Diner, my hair in a braid, wearing that horrible polo. It's a profile, and my lips are full and lush as I bite on my bottom lip. I look so . . . beautiful and achingly young.

My heart thunders.

The next three drawings are all of me.

One of me with a copy of *Jane Eyre* in my hand.

One of my naked back with my face hidden, the focus on the butterfly tattoo with his cell number inside the wings.

Finally, there's one of me outside his apartment building in Dallas, sitting on the park bench. My face is upturned as if I'm looking for him and I have my school uniform on.

I clench my small beaded handbag, emotion whipping through me, and instinctively I move on, needing to see how this ends.

The next few pass in a blur though I study each one, each one a depiction of himself.

Spider doing a line off a small mirror.

Spider's head on a table with a bottle of whiskey next to him.

Raw and real.

I struggle to contain my feelings. I can't break down here, not when this isn't really about me. It's about *him*.

I come to the end, another self-portrait of him looking into a mirror, his guitar strapped on his back. His hand rakes through his hair and his face is sharp and lean, his eyes open and clear. It's entitled *Recovery*.

I wipe at my eyes and head to the restroom just off to the side, avoiding everyone. Standing in front of the sink, I wipe at my face, and once I've gotten my mascara straightened out, I wash my hands, still teetering on losing control.

I have to see him. I have to tell him that I don't care if he can't say the words, I want to be with him anyway.

I don't even know he's followed me into the restroom until I raise my head to grab a tissue.

"Rose."

I turn to face him, whipping around and sucking in my breath.

He looks incredibly handsome in black slacks and a gray sweater. A leather cuff is on his wrist and a silver necklace hangs around his neck, accentuating his tan skin and the highlights in his dark hair, but it's his eyes that have most of my attention.

There's need in them.

"You paid for me to go to college? And Oscar?" I don't know why those are the first words out of my mouth instead of a compliment about his art, but since Robert handed over the folder, I've been in shock.

He gives me a short nod as he leans against the doorjamb and crosses his arms.

I shake my head at him, recalling the contents of the folder, the little things that had surprised me. "You made sure I got into the Krav Maga classes even though the waitlist was ridiculous and you even called the owner of Bono as soon as I applied for a job?"

He nods.

I swallow, feeling emotion tearing at me. "I used to wonder why I was so lucky in New York." I bite my lip. "How did you keep up with me?"

He exhales, his eyes scrutinizing my face, memorizing it. "For a while I had someone watching you periodically . . . nothing intrusive . . . just to make sure you were okay. Robert would keep me updated about things you wanted or mentioned, and I'd try to make it happen for you. It wasn't anything big."

"Why not let Robert pay for NYU?" I feel like he would have.

"*I* wanted to do something for you, Rose. I worked for that money and it was mine. I wanted you to be happy and have your friend with you." Anguish crosses his face. "I hurt you so much."

"Why do all this?" I ask, spreading my hands.

He smiles, though just barely, as if it hurts to do anything more. "I think you know why."

I nod.

His chest expands as his eyes sweep over me, and I know what he sees: a girl who dressed just for him. My dress is pure white, a slinky backless number that clearly shows my tattoo with my long hair up in elaborate curls. The skirt is a ridiculously short bit of tulle that flounces against my thighs when I walk in my silver stilettos.

"You're beautiful."

His words are like a balm to my soul.

"Thank you."

He comes closer and touches my face gently as if he's afraid I might vanish.

I close my eyes.

God.

I want to be his everything.

I want him to be consumed with me.

I want to be the person who keeps him on the straight and narrow.

I want him to not be able to get out of fucking bed unless I'm next to him.

I want him to crumble if I walk away.

I want him to love me forever.

I say those things to him as tears run down my face.

His face looks broken as he falls to his knees.

"Rose, I've been thinking about what you said. It's always been my intention to get you back someday, but everyone always leaves me," he says, his voice low. "The day Father dropped me off in Texas, I swore I'd be cold and hard and ruthless for the rest of my days. I swore to never let anyone rip my heart out, but then you came along . . . and I got so fucking lost in you."

I touch his cheek and he leans into me, his lips brushing my hand.

"I didn't admit it to myself until I was on the plane to LA, but I fell in love with you the moment we kissed, but I was a fucked up mess, and I didn't deserve you. I couldn't drag you down with me. I had to give you a real life without me, had to give you something so when we met again, you'd know I was ready for forever."

"You've been my forever since I was eleven." I drop to my knees in front of him.

He takes a deep breath and wetness shimmers in his intense gaze. "*I love you*, Rose, more than anything. I'm sorry I didn't say it earlier. If you still want me, if you still want us, then I'm right here."

My heart flies.

"Of course I still want you. I love you," I whisper. "I can't go on another single day without us together. I'm sorry for needing to hear those silly words. All we need is each other—"

He kisses me, cutting me off, his lips clinging to mine.

"Forever," he says in my ear.

And it was . . .

EPILOGUE

Spider

A few years later

"SIR, YOU CAN'T CARRY THAT on the plane."

I arch my brow at the ticketing agent. She's around fifty with a halo of blonde hair and bright pink lipstick. Normally, I can make any female do my bidding with my cocky grin and fancy English accent, but truth be told, I don't try as hard as I used to.

"Indeed."

She nods.

Her nametag says her name is Gwendolyn, and I smile, even though I'm beat from the three-month tour we just wrapped up in New York.

"Gwendolyn . . . may I call you Gwen?"

She blinks. "No."

I'm not fazed. I lean in and prop my arms on the counter, giving her a great view of my muscled biceps in the short-sleeved

Vital Rejects shirt I'm wearing. I've been working out daily, and I'm not ashamed to share my beautiful muscles with the world. "The truth is, I can't live without Helene—that's the name of my guitar." I glance down at the case at my feet. "She's been with me since the beginning of, well, everything, and it's bad luck to travel without her. Plus, I'm utterly exhausted, and if I don't have my guitar . . . I might be sad."

The agent gives me a onceover, her eyes lingering on the sweptback hair, which is white this month. "Do I know you?"

I grin. "You like British rock stars?"

"Not especially."

"Beautiful men with tattoos?" I twist my neck so she can see the spider.

Her nose turns up a notch. "Definitely not."

I smirk. "How about gritty music with incredible guitar riffs?"

She compresses her lips. "Don't want none of that stuff that makes my ears hurt. I listen to Kenny Rogers and Dolly Parton."

My eyes flare and I freeze—Dolly freaks me the hell out. Maybe it's the hair, maybe it's the boobs, but just the mention of her evokes mental images of her hiding behind a door or a shower curtain with a knife. I don't know why. I can't explain the fear; it just is.

"Need some help, baby?" Rose whispers from behind me, so close that her breath fans against the back of my neck. Just the sound of her voices relaxes me and makes me want to turn around and kiss her, but I have to focus. I'm determined to win this ticket agent over.

"No," I hiss under my breath. "I got this."

She laughs. Before arriving at the desk, we bet on whether or not I'd be able to get Helene on the plane with us. Usually we travel first class and it's not an issue to put the case in the coat closet, but when you're in coach, everything's different. Granted, I could have just checked her, but it bugs me if she isn't close.

"Sir," Gwendolyn says, eyeing me dismissively as she looks over my shoulder. "If you'll move along, I can get to the next person."

I try again, flashing a bright smile and waggling my brows. "In case you didn't know, I'm Spider from the Vital Rejects. Our fifth album just went double platinum."

"Never heard of you." She scrunches her nose.

Bloody hell. Leave it to me to get the person who doesn't know music.

From behind me, Rose laughs, reminiscent of the time when we met on a plane all those years ago. "Aren't you going to make up some lie about your girlfriend cheating on you with someone—oh, or maybe a dead dog?"

I answer her with, "My girlfriend—also known as my *wife*— would never cheat on me. She's happy with what she's got, if you must know. Her husband is fucking amazing."

"Is he now?" Rose says.

"It's no secret he's a stand-up mate, plus a stallion in the bed-room."

"Yes, he is," she murmurs. "And I love him."

Deep satisfaction falls over me. "Do you love me enough to handle this old bird? I don't think she cares for my looks, my tat-toos, or my music."

"Are you talking to yourself, sir?" the agent finally asks, her brow pulled down low over beady eyes. She's been eyeballing me since I started talking to Rose without actually turning around. I guess I do look weird. "Do I need to call security?"

I blink. Security? *Shit.* I really have lost this bet. I exhale, per-turbed that I can't get a guitar on a plane anymore.

"Let me handle her," declares Rose as she brushes past me, her heart-shaped arse swaying in all the right ways as she steps in front of me in her black halter dress. It's summer and her legs are bare and tan, and her copper hair is twisted up in some topknot that looks messy and stylish at the same time. With a determined look on her face, she marches up to the desk.

I grin and watch as she does what she does best: reading people and knowing exactly how to gauge their reactions. Her skills come in handy as our tour publicist for the band, focusing primarily on big media spots when we're on the road. Mila, who recently got married, still does our general PR, but she doesn't travel with us.

Rose fishes around in her bag, pulls out her phone, and shows something on it to Gwen—who has decidedly changed her tune and is smiling from ear to ear.

Wait . . .

What's going on?

I lean over to see Rose showing her photos of Chloe and Connor, our one-year-old twins.

"They're adorable!" she says, cooing at a picture of them playing in Central Park just a few days ago.

Rose smiles. "I know." She nudges her head at me. "And this cocky rock star is their dad."

Gwendolyn gives me a critical eye, but I think I see a softening there. "Is he a good one?"

I smirk and just stand back to wait for Rose's answer. We've been together for the past four years, and every single moment has been a dream. We went through hell getting it figured out all those years ago, but now that I'm clean, our fates have aligned.

"He's the best father ever," she murmurs softly, her hand over her heart.

Nice touch, my eyes say.

I learned from the best, hers say back.

Rose clears her throat and focuses back on Gwendolyn. "So if you can find a spot for the guitar in a coat closet or storage, that would be fantastic. Normally, we fly first class, but we brought along some friends to take to London and we all decided to fly coach together."

"We're packed, and the closet is probably already full." Gwendolyn thinks about it, her face doubtful.

"Made it! Thank God!" Oscar calls as he rushes over to us, pushing the twins in a double stroller. Wearing his black duster, he looks flustered. Axe trails behind him, smiling.

"You didn't mention that these little devils are disgusting with their poo. Oh my God, out of control," Oscar exclaims, his face pale as he glances down at them. "They're so . . . angelic-looking. I mean, it doesn't make sense."

I slap him on the shoulder and laugh. "You've had them for ten minutes, mate."

"Ten minutes is a lot when you can't breathe for fear of gagging."

"Is he your nanny?" Gwendolyn asks Rose.

Oscar rolls his eyes and waves at her. "Lord no. I'm the best friend. We're all going to London for a vacation at their new country home."

Axe raises a hand. "I'm the fiancé," he tells a blinking Gwendolyn.

Just then Chloe lets out a bloodcurdling yell and her face turns an *I demand to be picked up* red.

Before I can do it myself, Rose scoops her up and soothes her, patting her on the bottom as she bobs her up and down. I watch them, emotion tugging at me. As if she senses me thinking about her, Rose's green eyes shift away from Chloe and find mine. I get a buzz from the connection that's always been between us, that knowledge that she and I are two parts of a whole. I let out an exhale.

I'm nothing without this.

Without her.

Connor, the quiet one, looks up at me with his big brown eyes, and because I'm itching to be close to him, I pick him up and hold him.

Gwendolyn melts at the sight. I didn't do it to win the bet, but she picks up her phone and starts calling around, and in just a few seconds we have a flight attendant helping us with the stroller and the guitar, which they manage to find room for in the coat closet.

A few minutes later, we're seated with Rose and me next to each other. She holds Chloe and I have Connor. Oscar and Axe's seats are behind us, and I feel like I'm on top of the world.

It's just a simple day, but it's the little moments that mean the most, the ones that shape the fabric of our lives.

I think back to the past and how hard it was to get to this level of love.

I did self-destructive things and hurt people, and I can't go back and untangle the knot I made, but the past is the past, and now . . . I have a future.

I have Rose.

I have a family that loves me.

I lean over and kiss Rose, just like I did eight years ago, only this time we each have a child in our lap. I stare into her smiling eyes and know that she's my rock. "You're my everything," I say softly. "I love you."

She glows, happiness in her gaze. "Epic love . . . you and me."

The End

Dear Reader,

Thank you so much for reading Spider! Book reviews mean everything to indie authors, and if you have a moment, I'd appreciate an honest, heartfelt review. Just a few lines will do!

Also please join my Unicorn Girls reader group on Facebook. We talk smack and love unicorns. What else is better?

Xoxo,
Ilsa Madden-Mills

For more information about the next book,
please visit my social media sites:

www.ilsamaddenmills.com
www.amazon.com/Ilsa-Madden-Mills
www.facebook.com/authorilsamaddenmills
www.instagram.com/ilsamaddenmills
www.twitter.com/ilsamaddenmills
www.goodreads.com

BOOKS BY
ILSA MADDEN MILLS

Dirty English
Filthy English
Fake Fiancée
The Last Guy

BRIARWOOD ACADEMY SERIES:
Very Bad Things
Very Wicked Beginnings
Very Wicked Things
Very Twisted Things

ABOUT THE AUTHOR

WALL STREET JOURNAL BEST-SELLING AUTHOR Ilsa Madden-Mills writes about strong heroines and sexy alpha males that sometimes you just want to slap. She's addicted to dystopian books and all things fantasy, including unicorns and sword-wielding females. She has a degree in English and a Master's in Education.

Sign up for her newsletter to receive a FREE Briarwood Academy novella plus get insider info and exclusive giveaways!

www.ilsamaddenmills.com

ACKNOWLEDGEMENTS

THERE ARE SO MANY FANTASTIC people in the indie world that made this journey possible. Please know that my gratitude in no way lessens as the list continues.

For my husband who has stood by me every step of the way. You and me, babe, against the world.

For Lisa N. Paul—thank you for all the giggles and lunch dates that we've never had in person—except for the grits! Thank you for your phone calls and summer visits. Most of all thank, you for being my dear friend and being there every single day.

For Tia Louise, my twin brain, my signing buddy—thank you for the friendship, advice, and encouragement. I can't imagine a mermaid without thinking of you. Just keep swimming . . .

For Tijan—thank you for knowing when I need encouragement. I adore you.

For Caitlin (C. Marie)—thank you for being sweet and fast with line and copy.

For Jena Camp of Indie Girl Promotions and Lisa N Paul—thank you for the constructive content notes and advice.

For Julie Deaton, Erin Toland, and Stacy Nickelson—thank you for proofreading and helping me polish.

For Christine Borgford of Type A Formatting for doing a phenomenal job with formatting.

For Miranda Arnold of Red Cheeks Reads: my wonderful and talented PA. HOLLA! So happy we connected through our love of *Very Bad Things*. Thank you for being a go-getter for me. Race to the end, baby!

For the admin girls of Racy Readers: Erin Fisher, Tina Morgan, Elizabeth Thiele, Miranda Arnold, Stacy Nickelson, Heather Wish, Pam Huff, and Suzette Salinas. Thank you for your constant support, ideas, and love.

For Jenn Watson and the ladies at Social Butterfly PR, you are amazing! Thank you for holding my hand.

For my Unicorn Girls: you may be last on this list, but you are the BEST. You picked me up when I got knocked down and made me laugh. Thank you all for every shout out and each review you posted. Thank you for sharing a part of yourself in our group.

57006074R00148

Made in the USA
San Bernardino, CA
16 November 2017